Barnacle Child

A True Relation of Certain Events at Greyhook

David Horn

Sea Dreams Books

First edition, 2026

Print ISBN: 979-8-9994266-4-2

Cover design by David Horn

Cover art by Wajiha Kousar

Published by **Sea Dreams Books**
www.seadreamsbooks.net

For information about permissions, rights, or special editions, contact the publisher.

Contents

For those who know
that not every return is mercy.

"The sea may hear grief faster than God does, but it has no mercy in the answer." - *Seumas mac Dhòmhnaill*, c. 1824

What follows is not a single telling, but the form left by many.

Some of it was spoken and written at the time, some gathered later from those who remembered, and some taken from papers kept without much order until they were needed. Where the accounts do not agree, they are left so. Where names were avoided, they remain avoided.

This is not set down to make a better story of it, nor to correct what was already corrected before daylight, but to keep the sense of what occurred from being worn smoother than it should be.

Prologue

From the recollections of Seumas mac Dhòmhnaill, coastal catechist and lay reader & Taken down in English from his speech by A. R. Calder, schoolmaster, c. 1824

You'll hear many tellings of that matter if you sit long enough by the right fire and keep your mouth shut more than open, but there are not many I would trust completely. Folk trim a tale to suit themselves. They make it grander, cleaner, and, most often, safer. That is the way of people. They would rather have a lie they can sleep with than a truth that sits up in the room with them.

But this much was told to me by my mother's mother, and to her by someone even nearer to the thing itself. Though names were lost, the shape of it was not, and that is often the truer part.

It was before the kirk stood where it does now, before the burying-ground was set in proper order, before the road inland was much more than a track men cursed in wet weather. There were houses there then, aye, but poor ones, and not all where the houses are now. Some were nearer the inner reach, some farther up from the harbor mouth, and some, they said, were built where older footings were found under the sod, though no one could tell whose footings they had been. There were marks on a few stones, cuts in old timber, and the Christians who came later had no use for them but did not break them all, which was maybe wisdom and maybe fear.

There was a woman in that place, young enough still that folk would call her young, though sorrow had taken hold of her early. She had one son and no husband living. Whether he was drowned before that or taken by fever, I was never told plain, only that she had already given the sea and the land their share between them, and this boy was what remained in her arms of her own making.

Then the child became ill in the winter.

It was a bitter season, though not the worst. Do not believe a teller who says it was the worst of all, for such men are in love with bigness and have no care for truth. It was hard enough. The fish were poor. The wind held wrong for days on end. Frost crept into the pails indoors. Children coughed in the night until mothers sat up with both hands knotted in the blankets, listening to hear whether the next breath would come right or not.

The boy burned with fever, then went completely still afterward. That is how it was said. Burned, then still.

They washed him, wrapped him, and laid him out as they could. The ground was frozen hard then, and there would be no burying till men could get a spade to bite. So they watched with him in the house, as was right, though watching often turns to nodding when grief and weariness have had their way with a body.

In the black end of the night, the mother rose and took him up.

She made no cry. There was no calling out. She lit no candle.

There was only the lifting and the going.

And there was another woman wakeful then, an elder one, not old by count maybe, but old in the things that matter more. She had the look of one who had already buried what she loved and had learned not to ask the world to be fair after that. She saw movement beyond the window where no movement ought to have been, and she knew at once it would be no harmless thing. So she threw a shawl over herself and went after.

The younger woman had taken the path toward the outer shelf on the headland. You know the sort of place. Black rock. Bad footing in frost. The sea below not raging, not doing anything so simple as raging, but drawing and waiting. There are coasts where danger comes at you plain. There are others where it bides. That was such a coast.

The moon was up enough to give a mean light over everything. Boats lay above the storm-line white at the edges with frost. The sheds were all black backs and crooked roofs. The snow had an old crust on it where the wind had worried it into hardness. A cruel, listening kind of night.

The elder woman followed till she saw the younger one standing on the lower rock with the child in her arms.

And she heard her speaking low and level, as one speaks to something that is listening close and has no need of loudness.

She said, "You've had enough."

That much was remembered all the years after.

Then she said, "You'll not keep him and call it winter."

Now think on that. A woman may cry against God in her grief. Many have. A woman may curse the season, the fever, the hunger, the doctor, the whole hard make of the world. But this was not that. She was speaking as if there were an ear in the sea and a reckoning in it too. As if winter itself were only the name men gave to a taking that belonged to something deeper and older and nearer at hand.

The elder woman called to her then. "Come back," she said. "Come away from there."

But the younger one did not come.

And the sound of the water changed.

I do not mean to say that it grew louder. That would be easy. It changed.

Those who have lived long by the sea know there are many sounds in water, and each has its own meaning if you have the wit to hear it. There is breaking, and sucking, and under-pull, and wash over stone, and tide between pilings, and the knock of driftwood, and the small mean slap of harbor water in calm. This was none of those things, though there was some likeness to all of those things. It was as if the water had drawn one breath inward and was holding it.

The elder woman went down as far as she dared, and no farther. She had sense enough for that.

She said, "Do not speak again."

And the younger one answered, "It knows me."

That was bad.

Then she said, "It knows what's mine."

That was worse.

For there are things a grieving soul may say that are not prayers at all, though spoken in want and love, and one of the worst of them is to lay claim before the dark and ask the dark to answer in the same language.

The elder woman said to her, "Aye, and for that very reason you'll not give it leave."

That saying I have always thought a wise one.

Below them and beyond, the black water turned pale in one place where no wave was breaking. No foam. No crest. Only a whitening, as if something down in the depth had shifted its side toward the moon. Some said later there were shapes there like timbers under flood. Some said not. I was not there, and I'll not lie for the sake of a stronger tale. But all agree there was wrongness in the water, and wrongness enough to be known.

Then came the thing most fearful.

The child moved.

Do not ask me whether it was life. I say only what was said: he moved. A stir under the wrappings. No more than that. A settling, a drawing-in, a twitch no mother in that hour could have borne with sense.

And the young woman bent over him at once and crooned to him as if he had only waked poor from sleep.

Then the elder one did what needed doing, which is often not the soft thing and not the thing thanked for after. She went to her, laid hold of her hard, and told her plain:

"That is not for you. What answers from there does not return what was taken. It only puts a hand through the door."

That is how it was given to me.

Not everyone says it the same, but that is the heart of it.

The mother fought her then, I think, though only a little and only because grief can turn even love into rage when it is crossed. But the elder woman was stronger in the soul if not in the body, and she spoke on, saying there had been folk on that coast before theirs — not kirk folk, not folk under any minister, but sea-taught folk who had left warnings in marks and ways and names half-buried now. She said the coast had been instructed before their own people came to build there, and that some places were never to be asked twice.

At last the mother yielded.

She gave over the child into the elder woman's arms and fell down on her knees upon the stone, not as in prayer exactly, but as if something inside her had gone out all at once and left the body with no proper work to do but kneel.

And the sea, having had no leave from her, settled back into its common speech.

That is always the wicked comfort of such things. Once denied, they go ordinary again. They leave behind no great sign a magistrate could take hold of. No wound. No mark. Nothing but shaken people and a story already beginning to be corrected before daylight.

By the morning, it had been turned into a better tale.

She had wandered, they said.

She was not in her full mind, they said.

The elder woman found her before harm was done, they said.

Aye.

And because people are made the way they are, that became the story fit for keeping.

But other things were kept too, though not in open speech.

After that, the dead were watched close till burial.

Children were not carried toward the headland in winter dark.

On certain turn-tide nights a bowl of brine was put under the bed, especially where there had been sickness or mourning.

And among the oldest sort there was a saying, quiet and seldom before strangers:

The sea may hear grief faster than God does, but it has no mercy in the answer.

That is the tale as I had it.

Whether the first folk there were Norse, heathen, or only hungry men with better ears than ours, I cannot tell you. I have heard too much foolishness from both proud scholars and proud fools on that matter. There were older marks on that coast than the settlers made. That I believe. There were warnings before the Book had them. That, too, I believe. But names are cheap things to lay over fear. People are always wanting to name what should first be obeyed.

So take from the account whatever good sense you may.

A mother in grief is nearer to bargaining than she knows.

A coast remembers lessons the people upon it forget.

And what speaks back from black water does not love the living, though it may know well enough how to sound like it does.

1

The Returning Shore

By the time the boats appeared at the Mouth, the village had already decided they were late enough to merit discussion but not yet late enough to be mourned. That was the way of Greyhook with danger. As long as a thing could still be named delay, inconvenience, bad weather, poor judgment, or a lesser cousin to calamity, folk clung to that smaller word and used it hard. Only after the sea had stripped away every modest name a loss might wear did they allow themselves to say what had happened.

When word came down from the wharf that Tam Bain's boat had been seen beyond the black arm of rock, no one shouted deliverance. Men came out of sheds drying brine and scales from their hands. Women looked up from the baskets of gutting and mending and stood in doorways gripping aprons twisted in fists. Boys ran for half news and half because running always made all news feel better for a minute. When Bain's boat nosed through the narrow cut of the harbor's mouth, three lanterns had been lit against the lowering dark, and a fourth lantern was being argued over.

"Waste the oil if you like," Mrs. Kincaid called from beside the fish table, not looking up from the cod she was cleaning. "They'll not row any cleaner for more light."

But she was smiling when she said it, even as she wiped her hands and turned.

It had been an ugly day from first light: low clouds, an easterly wind that came in long, damp strokes, and water outside the harbor, thick-looking and mean. Not a storm, not enough for prayer or shutters, only the sort of weather that settled into the bones and made a man short-tempered with his own buttons. By afternoon, a raw mist had begun to gather off the water, enough to soften every line and smear distances into one another. The whole village had taken on that muffled look of a place half decided not to show itself.

Mairi Bain stood back a little from the others near the main wharf, her shawl pulled close, one hand tucked under her opposite elbow as if bracing herself against the wind. She had come down when the call went out, as anyone would. No one had expected her to remain in the house. But she had chosen a place neither among the men waiting to tie lines nor among the women already speaking of broth and dry stockings, and of what poor fools chose a day like this to stay out longer than they must. She stood where she could see both the Mouth and the harbor. It was an old habit with her, though she would not have called it that. Since Ewan had gone overboard in August, she found herself measuring every return against the one that never happened.

Tam's boat came in with two men bent hard to the oars and Tam himself at the stern, broad as a gate even at a distance, his sou'wester dark with spray. The craft rode lower than Mairi liked to see, though whether it was from catch or weather she could not yet tell. There was no cheer at first, not quite. Greyhook did not cheer early. But the collective held breath loosened a little.

"About time," someone muttered.

"Aye, and a poor shape coming in too," another answered.

"Poor shape is better'n no shape."

That drew a few grim sounds that might have been laughter.

The boat crossed the Mouth properly, taking the familiar turn between Crowe's Ledge and the black post at the harbor lip. Tam knew every mood of that entrance and more than one it had no right to have. Even in mist, even with the tide on the move, he handled her as if the boat were being led along old lines cut into the water for him alone.

Mairi watched him without warmth.

Tam Bain. Her husband's brother. The man who had returned in August with rope burn on one palm, salt in the creases of his eyes, and a face so carefully kept that she had known, before he opened his mouth, there would be no comfort in what he said.

He had stood in this same harbor, telling her the boy went over too quickly, too quickly, the line fouled, the footing bad, the sea ugly in a way no one had expected. He had said all the right things in the right order. Men had nodded. Women had lowered their eyes. The minister had come by before dusk.

None of it had made Ewan appear.

So now, seeing Tam bring his boat safely in, Mairi felt not relief but something harder to confess: a resentment so old it had become part of her grain.

The hull bumped into wood. Lines were thrown, caught, and tied fast. Men stepped forward, shoulders set to the ordinary work of docking. The smell of fish rose thick from the boat then—cod, mostly, and something oily beneath it—and with it came the harsher smell of wet rope, bilge, salt, and men who had been too long in the weather. Tam climbed up from the stern and gave his shoulders a hard shake, like a dog coming in from the rain.

"Well?" Mr. Reid called.

"Well enough," Tam said. "If you'd like to call two split nets, one fouled hook-line, and a catch half what ought to be well."

"Then you've had a profitable day by the sound of it."

That drew a rough laugh. More men pressed closer. Hands went to crates and baskets. The easy, practiced exchange of labor began.

Mairi might have turned away then. There was no reason to linger. Tam was back; the village had its proof against the dark for one more evening; the business at the wharf would settle into sorting, tallying, cursing, and hauling before long. She had potatoes to peel, the stove to feed, and an empty house that had never yet grown any easier to enter at dusk.

She had already begun to turn when the child screamed, farther off, down the beach beyond the wharf, where the shingle sloped away from the harbor works toward the open edge of the tide. It was a shrill, full-bodied scream, the kind that tears itself free before sense can reach it.

Everything stopped.

That was what Mairi remembered later, more than the scream itself: the pause after it. A net half-lifted between two men. Mrs. Kincaid's knife held in the air above a fish spine. A gull flapping up from a piling as if the whole harbor had jerked beneath it.

"What now?" Tam barked, already turning.

The boy who had screamed—wee Alec Crowe, all elbows and bad judgment—stood near the beach's edge with one hand flung up as though warding something off. He did not point. He only stared.

Heads turned in the same direction.

At first, Mairi saw nothing but the usual evening confusion: wet stone, the pale wrack-line, the last ragged wash of tide, and mist dragging itself low over the farther reach of shore. Then a shape separated itself from the dark beyond the shingle.

Someone whispered, "Who's that?"

No one answered.

The figure stood where the sea reached and withdrew from his feet without seeming to move. Bareheaded. Barefoot. Too still.

For one senseless instant, Mairi thought some boatman from farther down the coast had come ashore, drunk or injured, and had lost his wits enough to stand looking in at the village as if he could not decide whether he knew it. Then the wind shifted enough to bring the figure's face into a little clearer view under the lantern-light and the torn remains of day.

Mairi saw the line of a cheek. The slight tilt of the head. The narrowness through the shoulders. The old scar at the corner of the mouth, where he had fallen against a nail at five and carried the mark afterward like a bad boast.

The world did not narrow, as people say. It widened too quickly, and everything in it seemed to pull away from her at once.

"Ewan," she said.

It came out no louder than breath.

Then, louder and already moving, "Ewan!"

She did not know afterward whether she had shoved people aside or whether they had leaped out of her way before she reached them. She knew only that there were hands, coats, and voices between her and the shore one instant and none the next. Her boots slipped once on weed-dark stone at the edge of the wharf slope, and she caught herself with one palm hard against a piling, then drove on.

Behind her, someone said, "Dear God."

Someone else: "It can't be."

Tam's voice, nearer than she wanted it: "Mairi—"

She did not hear the rest.

The boy at the tide line turned his head slowly toward her. That motion alone ought to have broken her, for it was his. It was the way of it: careful, as if he had always listened with his whole neck, not just his ears. Ewan had done that since infancy, angling himself toward sound rather than snapping to it like some children did. It had been one of the hundred little things a mother knew, never once expecting it to matter.

It mattered now.

She reached him and stopped short by no more than a hand's breadth.

He was taller than when he had gone out in August, or perhaps only thinner. The rags hanging from him—shirt or undershirt once, trousers stiff with salt and wear—clung in strips and folds that made no proper shape. His hair lay in pale, dark ropes against his skull, longer now, full of grit and salt. One side of his face was crusted with something that caught the weak light dully.

Not seaweed. Not dried mud. Not any harmless thing.

His skin had changed. At the throat first, where a mother's eye goes quickest. Along the hollow above the collarbone, a ridge of pale growth ran, layered like shell against shell, not laid on him but rising from him. Smaller clusters marked the line beneath one ear and trailed under the jaw. One wrist showed a rough circlet of the same stuff where his sleeve had torn away. Not barnacles exactly, not as she had seen them on hulls and pilings all her life. Nearer to that than to anything else, but fused too close, too intimate, the ridged edges lying against flesh with the assurance of belonging.

Mairi's stomach turned once, hard, then settled into a cold steadiness that frightened her more.

"Ewan," she said again, and now the name broke.

He looked at her. His eyes were open and clear. There was no fever in them, no wandering, no ordinary ruin of a child lost at sea and somehow cast back whole. If he had been wild with hunger, shattered with fright, or witless from exposure, she might have known where to put her hands and which prayer to choose. But he only looked at her with a stillness so complete it seemed not calm but depth.

She reached out.

Someone behind her said, "Don't touch him."

She did not know who. She turned her head half an inch, enough to say without looking, "Be still."

Then she laid her hand against her son's cheek.

It was cold. Not the cold of the wind, nor even the cold of a wet child dragged from the surf. It was the cold of stone beneath deep water. The cold of something that had not seen the sun in a long time and did not miss it. But it was flesh beneath her palm. Flesh and bone and the familiar shape of him. She felt the old scar by his mouth under her thumb. Felt the angle of his jaw, sharper now. Felt the slight tremor that ran through him, not from shivering but from some slower inner strain she could not name.

"Oh, my dear God," she whispered.

His mouth opened.

Mairi bent close at once. "Aye. Aye, speak, then. I'm here. Speak to me."

Nothing came. Not a rasp. Not the ruined croak of a throat too long unused. Not even air with intention in it. His lips parted. The tongue moved once. Silence remained.

Behind her, the village had inched nearer. She could feel them now at her back: their fear, their pity, their greed for an explanation, all blended into that particular Greyhook hush that meant everyone was listening and no one wanted to be the first to say the wrong thing aloud.

Tam stepped up on her left. She could tell by the shape of him in the corner of her sight.

"Mairi," he said carefully, "come away a little."

She turned then, slowly enough that the movement felt borrowed from her son.

"Come away from my son?"

Tam's face was blanched under weather and beard. For the first time since August she saw something in him that did not fit any of the practiced expressions he had worn since the loss: neither endurance, nor guilt, nor the brisk practicality men use when they cannot mend what has happened and mean to survive it anyway.

This was fear.

That did more to steady her than kindness would have.

"Get a blanket," she said.

Mrs. Kincaid startled as if struck. "Aye. Aye, of course."

"And send for Dr. Calder."

Mr. Reid muttered, "From Little Narrows? At this hour?"

"At whatever hour he is reached," Mairi said, not raising her voice. "You have a cart, and if you've not, then take Tam's horse."

Tam began, "Mairi—"

She rounded on him so fast that even Ewan's stillness did not hold her back from it.

"You'll not tell me what cannot be done tonight."

Something passed across Tam's face then—shame, anger, or some old pain too stale to distinguish. But he did not argue.

Mrs. Kincaid came hurrying with a blanket from one of the sheds, muttering to herself the way people did when frightened and busy at once. Mairi took it and wrapped it round Ewan's shoulders. He neither helped nor resisted. When she drew the coarse wool close at his throat she had to work it carefully around the pale ridged growth there. Her fingers shook only once, and she was glad of the failing light to hide it.

"Can you walk?" she asked him.

His gaze moved past her then, not far, only toward the harbor. Toward the pilings and dark water under the wharf where the tide shifted in and out of the inner reach.

Mairi felt it before she heard it: a long, low creak through the wood underfoot. Not unusual in itself. Every harbor made noises. Greyhook's timbers spoke all day and night with load, weather, and tide. But this sound seemed to run beneath the others rather than among them. A wet inward drag, followed by a muted knock, as if something large and water-heavy had rolled itself against the buried roots of the place.

Others heard it too. Mairi knew because the hush deepened further, impossibly, and someone crossed himself before remembering where he stood.

Tam looked toward the wharf.

Old Ailie Crowe, who must have come down without Mairi seeing when the cry went up, said from behind the gathered villagers, "Do not make noise over it."

No one told her to hush, though in another mood several would have.

Mairi turned back to Ewan.

"Can you walk?"

This time he nodded once. A small motion. Obedient almost. That, more than all the rest, made her want to sink to the stones and take him in both arms and weep until she brought the village down around them. But she did not. There were too many eyes. There would be time enough for breaking if God proved cruel and gave her any.

She slipped one arm around him.

He was lighter than he ought to have been and heavier in strange places, as if the set of his balance had altered. When he took his first step from the wash of tide onto the rougher shingle above, he moved carefully, not from weakness exactly but from unfamiliarity, like a child new from illness learning his own limbs again. The blanket dragged at one side. His bare feet left dark wet marks that ought to have looked ordinary and did not.

The villagers fell back to let them pass. Mairi walked between them and did not look left or right. She felt them staring at the side of Ewan's face, at the shell-ridged throat beneath the blanket edge, at the marks on his wrist. She heard the little involuntary sounds people make when forcing themselves not to ask questions. She heard Tam order two boys to run for the cart road. She heard Mrs. Kincaid whisper, “Sweet Lord preserve us,” and someone answer, “From what?”

At the foot of the wharf slope, Old Ailie Crowe stood aside but did not move away. She was wrapped in a dark shawl, her hair mostly hidden beneath it, her face lined less by age than by weather and use. Her eyes were fixed on Ewan, but not with the startled helplessness of the others. Hers was an old, measuring look, the sort a person gives a split seam in a boat or a swelling place in a wall where one knows trouble by shape before one knows it by name.

Ewan stopped.

Mairi felt him do it before she saw why.

Old Ailie had looked down. In the wet sand at the edge of the path where the shingle gave way to packed earth, Ewan had left a print clearer than the rest. Not the outline of his foot alone. Within the wet dark there showed, just for an instant before the seep of water took it, a fine ribbed pattern like the underside of shell.

Ailie’s face did not change. That was its own kind of alarm.

“Get him indoors,” she said quietly.

Mairi’s hand tightened on the blanket at Ewan’s chest. “Aye. That was my thought.”

Ailie lifted her eyes to meet hers. “And shut the back room.”

Mairi stared at her.

"What for?"

"Because I said it."

Mairi might have snapped then—might have told the old woman to mind her own hearth, her own mending, her own muttered wisdom no one asked after in daylight. But Ailie's gaze had shifted past her shoulder to the harbor again, and there was something in that look Mairi did not like at all.

She turned. The water under the wharf had gone dark as iron in the failing light. A length of weed rolled slowly on the inner tide. One of the tied boats rocked once against its line and settled.

Nothing there.

Nothing to be named.

Nothing a sensible woman would stop over.

Yet Mairi heard, or thought she heard, from somewhere inside the timbered bones of the wharf and the houses above it, a soft inward pull. Not wave. Not wind.

A tide.

Inside the wood.

She looked down at Ewan.

He was listening too. His face had turned slightly toward the sound, and for the first time since she had seen him at the shore, some expression crossed it—not fear, not comfort, but recognition so faint and terrible it might have been mistaken for simple attention by anyone who had not once held him newborn and learned every weather of his face before he had words.

Mairi drew the blanket tighter and set him moving again.

Up the slope. Past the sheds. Past the gathered mouths and lanterns and the smell of fish. Toward the house that had gone empty in August and now stood waiting with all its old boards and hidden seams.

Behind her Greyhook began at last to find its voice again. Low voices first. Then instructions. Then questions no one answered. Then the rough rattle of ordinary work taken up too loudly by people who wanted the comfort of sound.

But under it, and beneath the beat of her own blood, Mairi carried one certainty home with her through the darkening village:

The sea had given her son back.

It had not given him back kindly.

2

Shell Under Skin

Dr. Hugh Calder arrived in Greyhook after midnight with mud to the axles, temper gone thin, and one glove missing. The cart was heard before it was seen: wheels catching in the bad stretch below the kirk rise, harness leather straining, Tam's voice low and sharp to the horse, then the final wet jolt as they came into the village proper. By then Mairi had been listening for him so long that every sound had become him once before turning back into something else. A gust at the shutter. A loose board settling in the lean-to. A drag of current under the house where no such drag ought to be. Twice she had risen from the chair beside Ewan's bed certain she heard wheels. Twice she had opened the door to nothing but the lane, the dark, and the lamp in Mrs. Kincaid's far window.

The real arrival brought no relief with it. Only movement.

Tam came in first, stamping mud from his boots and filling the doorway with cold air. Dr. Calder followed with his black bag and a look already arranged for annoyance, the sort of look a man wears when summoned from sleep for some ordinary emergency he means to manage briskly and resent later. He was a lean man in his forties, dark-haired still though the temples were going, with a close beard and the hard, dry manner of one too often called to places where pain had outrun money.

"Mrs. Bain," he said, touching two fingers to the brim of his hat before he set it aside. "You'll forgive the hour."

"No." Mairi rose from the chair. "But I'll forgive the delay."

That startled the shadow of a smile out of him, gone quickly. Tam shifted at the door as if he might speak in warning, but Calder had already turned his head toward the small room beyond, where the lamp burned low.

"That's the boy?"

"My son," Mairi said.

"Aye."

He did not apologize for the first word. Mairi was glad of that. She had no room tonight for gentleness that meant nothing.

The back room of the house had always been the colder one. In winter the floorboards held chill no matter how well the stove in the kitchen was fed, and in summer the light reached it late and left it early. Since August Mairi had shut the door against herself more often than not. Ewan's bed was there still under the narrow window, the blanket box at the foot, the little shelf Tam had fixed badly two springs ago still leaning a touch to one side. She had entered the room every few days to air it, straighten what needed no straightening, and leave again before the smell of old soap and boy and unused boards could loosen something in her.

Now Ewan lay in his own bed beneath wool and patched quilt, his head turned a little toward the wall. He had made no complaint on the walk home. Nor any while she stripped the wet rags from him with hands that shook worst only once, at the first sight of the ridged shell growth continuing below the collarbones. None while she bathed what skin remained simply skin. None while she worked around the changed places and tried not to think of the fact that her son, missing at sea these three months, smelled not of rot, nor waste, nor hunger, but of salt and deep-cold stone and something faintly metallic beneath both.

He had taken broth badly, managing little. Water he would hold in his mouth a moment, then swallow as if remembering the use of his throat. He had not slept, so far as she could tell. But he had lain quiet, eyes opening and closing without true rest, listening always toward the wall.

Dr. Calder paused on the threshold.

Tam had told him something on the road. Mairi saw that at once. Not everything, perhaps—Tam's cowardice would not run that far—but enough that the doctor did not stride in with ordinary authority. He stood a moment taking measure of the room, the lamplight, the woman, the child, and the old woman in the corner.

Old Ailie Crowe had arrived not long after Mairi brought Ewan home and had not yet been made to leave. She sat near the stove-end of the kitchen with her shawl on and her hands folded under it, as if she had come only to warm herself and found no suitable moment to go. She had spoken little. Once only, asking Mairi whether there was older timber in the back wall. When Mairi demanded what business that was of hers, Ailie had said, "The sort that becomes everyone's once it begins," and gone silent again.

Now Calder saw her and gave the briefest inclination of his head.

"Mrs. Crowe."

"Doctor."

Nothing in either voice suggested welcome.

He crossed to the bed. Mairi moved with him and stopped on the other side, her hand going to the bedpost as if she needed the permission of wood to remain upright.

Calder looked down at Ewan a long moment before opening his bag.

"Well now," he said at last, but not to the child. To himself, perhaps. "Let's see what weather made of you."

Ewan's eyes opened, and for the first time since the beach, Mairi saw him take notice of a stranger as stranger. The doctor's face, voice, movement—something about the newness of them held him with that deep attention he had once given trapped crabs in rock pools, watching to see what their kind of life meant when left to itself.

"I'm Dr. Calder," the man said, as if introductions still belonged to the world. "I'd ask where you've been, lad, but your mother would strike me for wasting time."

Mairi said, "Try it and see."

This drew a more definite ghost of a smile from Calder, though his eyes stayed on the boy.

He began with the ordinary things. Pulse at the wrist. Eyelids lifted to inspect the pupils. Fingers pressing lightly along jaw and throat. A thermometer from his case. Questions asked not because answers were expected but because the sequence mattered.

"Can you hear me?"

No reply.

"Can you understand?"

Ewan's gaze moved once, following the sound of the doctor's voice but not settling long on his mouth.

"Any pain here?" Calder pressed gently along the forearm where no shell showed.

Nothing.

He shifted to the other arm. At the wrist the skin disappeared beneath a pale rough circlet of calcified ridges, clustered and overlapping like growth on harbor stone. Up close it was worse than on the shore. Not uglier, precisely.

More intimate. The edges vanished under flesh that had closed around them as if it had been taught to.

Calder touched the growth with one finger.

Ewan flinched.

Mairi leaned forward at once. "There. You saw."

"Aye."

"Then leave off."

"I touched him, Mrs. Bain."

"And he felt it."

"That is generally the hope in such cases."

"Not if you touch again where he's changed."

Calder straightened a little and looked across the bed at her. He was tired, cold, called out in the middle of the night, and standing in a room where a drowned boy ought not to be lying warm enough to trouble him. Mairi saw all that. Yet whatever sharpness rose in him died quickly.

"I'll be as gentle as I may."

"That is not what I asked."

"No," he said. "But it is what you're getting."

Ailie made a sound in her throat that might have been approval or warning. Tam, still hovering in the doorway between room and kitchen as if neither place would admit him entirely, said, "Doctor—"

"Either stand still or go out," Calder said without turning.

Tam stood still.

The thermometer came away. Calder held it to the lamp and frowned.

"Well?"

He glanced up at Mairi. "Cool."

"How cool?"

"Cooler than I'd like."

"That means nothing."

"It means his temperature's low."

"He's cold from the shore."

"He has been inside near five hours."

That silenced her, because it had not felt like five hours, though of course it must have been.

Calder put down the thermometer and reached for the blanket. "I need to see more of it."

Mairi's hand came down over his on the quilt.

"No."

He did not snatch his fingers away. "Mrs. Bain—"

"No."

"Then I'll tell you now I'll be guessing in the dark."

"Guess, then."

"On what I've seen already, I'd say exposure, severe privation, tissue damage of some strange sort—"

"Strange sort?" Mairi said. "Is that what men learn after all those books?"

His mouth thinned. "What would you prefer I call what's under his skin?"

Ailie said quietly from the kitchen, "Call it what it is when you know."

That turned him, briefly. "And do you?"

"No."

"Then we'll both practice humility."

Tam muttered, "Best of luck with that."

Calder ignored him. He looked back at Mairi's hand over his. "If I cannot examine him properly, I may as well go home."

"Then go."

Mairi said it because she could not bear the alternative: a stranger pulling back the blanket while all of Greyhook's wrongness gathered in the corners of the room to watch. But the moment the words left her she knew she did not mean them. Not entirely. She wanted the doctor gone. She wanted him to stay. She wanted him to lay one clean hand on the impossible and reduce it, if not to safety then at least to a name she could work against. She wanted him to fail quickly so she could hate him properly for it.

Calder seemed to understand some part of this. "Mrs. Bain," he said, not unkindly, "if your son was found as they tell me he was found, then there is no common sense in any of this. That does not free me from trying."

Under her palm his hand stayed still.

Mairi took hers away.

"Only enough," she said.

He nodded once and drew back the quilt.

The room changed. Mairi felt every person in the house turn inward toward the bed, as if the opening of cloth had opened something else with it.

Ewan lay on his back in the yellow light, his chest and shoulders bare.

The growth had spread farther than Mairi had seen in the hurried washing. It ran from the base of the throat in branching plates and clustered ridges, pale grey and faintly lustrous, not like dry shell but like shell taken live from tide pools and held a moment before it dulled. Along the left shoulder it thickened into a rough seam curving under the clavicle. Smaller nodes marked the ribs in a pattern too ordered to be random and too irregular to be called symmetrical. One patch near the sternum had the look of something layered there over time, as reefs build themselves by patient accretion.

The skin between the growths was not right either. It was not diseased in any way Mairi had ever seen. Rather it seemed thinned and altered in color, as if flesh that had expected one kind of pressure had been taught another.

Tam swore softly.

Calder said nothing.

It was Ailie who spoke first.

"Not barnacle."

"No," Calder said after a moment.

"What then?"

He leaned close, not touching. "Calcification," he said, but without conviction. "Some kind of mineral deposit. Tissue response, perhaps."

"To what?"

He did not answer.

Mairi's eyes had gone to one place low along Ewan's side where the shell gave way to skin just above the rib. There, half-hidden by shadow, she saw a ringed mark no wider than the mouth of a teacup, pale around the edge and darker within, as if something had attached there hard and long enough to leave its memory in him.

She reached toward it before she could stop herself.

Calder caught her wrist lightly. "Don't."

"Why?"

"Because I don't know what it is."

She looked at his hand on her and he let go at once.

He bent closer still. "Bring the lamp."

Tam moved before Mairi could. He took the lamp from the shelf and came near, holding it low. Yellow light deepened the shadows between the shell ridges. Calder narrowed his eyes.

"What?" Mairi asked.

"There."

He indicated the seam at the shoulder.

At first she saw only more of the same pale layering. Then one edge lifted slightly as Ewan breathed—or not breathed, she thought wildly, but moved in some other inward rhythm—and Mairi saw beneath it not bleeding flesh, not infection, not bone.

Pores. Tiny openings in the skin beneath the shell, arranged in a thin crescent. They opened and closed so faintly she might have thought it a trick of light, had Calder not gone very still and Tam not sucked air sharply through his teeth.

No one spoke.

The pores closed again. Opened. Closed.

Ailie rose from her chair in the kitchen.

"That room wants barring," she said.

Calder straightened, half turning. "What?"

"The room."

"For God's sake, Mrs. Crowe—"

"Bar it at the back wall."

"This is a child, not a storm-cellar."

"No," Ailie said. "Worse luck."

Mairi ignored them both. "Ewan."

His eyes shifted to her. He was awake. He was hearing. He was there.

She clung to that with everything in her.

"Ewan, does it hurt?"

His mouth parted.

Nothing. But his gaze slid, slowly and unmistakably, toward the wall beside the bed.

All of them looked.

The wall was just a wall: rough paper gone faded with years, a crack near the window frame, the old dark line where one winter's damp had once climbed and dried again. Nothing moving. Nothing visible.

Then, faint as the memory of a sound, there came from behind the plaster a soft inward wash.

Not a rat. Not settling timber. Not wind.

Water.

Mairi closed her eyes once.

"No," she said quietly.

The sound came again. A little stronger. A tide-lap, impossible and unmistakable, as though the sea had found some narrow way into the house and was feeling its reach.

Tam lowered the lamp by instinct, as if better light might help him against it. "You hear that?"

No one answered because all of them did.

Calder stepped to the wall and laid two fingers against it. The plaster was dry. He pressed harder, then rapped once with his knuckles. A mean, ordinary sound. He frowned and put his ear near the paper.

The tide-sound ceased.

He waited. So did the rest of them.

Nothing.

Calder drew back. "The house is old."

Tam let out an ugly little laugh. "Aye, and the sea's wet. Will you give us more wisdom?"

"It may be pipes."

"In this house?" Mairi said.

He glanced at her and conceded the point with a slight movement of the mouth.

Ailie had come nearer now, stopping short of the bed. She looked not at the wall but at the floor beneath it, then at the lintel, then the line of boards under the window.

"Older timber," she said.

Mairi almost struck her for the steadiness of her voice. "You said that before."

"And I was right before."

Tam rounded on her. "If you've something to say, woman, say it plain."

Ailie looked at him. "Plain truth is wasted on men after midnight."

"That'll do," Calder snapped, though whether to Tam or Ailie it was impossible to tell.

He returned to the bed and drew the quilt up again, carefully this time, with more gentleness than Mairi would have believed him capable of half an hour earlier.

"The growths should not be touched further tonight," he said. "Nor scraped, nor washed hard, nor covered wet. Keep him warm. Small sips only. Broth if he'll take it. Watch whether he passes water, whether he sleeps, whether the temperature rises or falls. If he grows restless or seizes, send for me at once."

"That's all?" said Mairi.

"For now."

"That's nothing."

"It is what I have."

"It is less than what I had before you came."

His tone stayed even. "Mrs. Bain, if your son had been hauled from a wreck this evening with common injuries, I might give you common comfort. He was not. I won't lie to make myself seem useful."

Ailie said, "That may be the first sound thing spoken in this house."

Tam exhaled through his nose like a bull readying.

Mairi sat down abruptly on the chair beside the bed because her knees had begun to shake and she would not sway before them. She took Ewan's hand above the shell-marked wrist and held it, feeling the strange coolness in him, the slight pulse there, the fact of him. It was all at once too much and not nearly enough.

Calder closed his bag.

"I'll come again at first light."

"Why?" Mairi asked without looking up.

He hesitated. "Because I've never seen the like. Because I should. Because if the condition changes, I'd rather observe it before someone in the village takes a knife to it."

Her head came up sharply.

"No one will touch him."

Tam said, "No one said—"

She turned on him with such force that he took a half step back. "No one will touch him."

Silence followed.

Then Ewan moved.

Only his fingers at first, tightening once around Mairi's hand.

She looked down.

His eyes were on the wall again.

The tide-sound returned, very softly. Not from far off now, but just behind the bedstead, as if the wood itself had taken to breathing in its sleep.

Mairi rose.

"Out," she said.

Calder blinked. "Mrs. Bain—"

"Out. All of you."

Tam stared. "You'd keep alone with—"

"My son."

Ailie, unexpectedly, obeyed first. She gathered her shawl and moved toward the door without a word. Calder looked from the bed to the wall to Mairi's face and seemed to think better of argument. He took his bag and followed. Tam was the last, slowest to go.

At the threshold he stopped.

"Mairi."

She did not answer.

His voice roughened. "Whatever happened on the boat that day—"

She turned then, and something in her face shut his mouth before the rest could come.

"Not tonight," she said.

Tam stood one second longer as if he had forgotten how doors worked. Then he went out, pulling it half closed behind him.

Mairi crossed the room and shut it properly. The latch settled. The house beyond muffled itself around her: one board creaking under someone's step, the low murmur of Calder's voice, Tam answering too fast, Ailie not answering at all. Then even that thinned.

Only Mairi and Ewan remained in the little room.

And the tide in the wall.

She stood listening to it, one hand on the latch, until the fear in her had nowhere left to climb and began at last to settle into something worse and more usable.

She went back to the bed and sat.

Ewan watched her.

"All right," she whispered, though nothing was. "All right then. It's only us."

At that, the strange calm in his face altered. Very slightly. Less than a smile. Less than relief. But enough that she saw he had understood.

Mairi reached and smoothed his hair back from his forehead. The motion was automatic, old as infancy. Beneath her other hand his fingers were still cold.

"Whatever the sea thinks it has done," she said quietly, "it has not finished with me first."

The tide-lap behind the wall went on in the dark wood, patient as breath.

And for the first time since the beach, Ewan closed his eyes as if sleep might come.

3

A Sound Behind the Plaster

By morning Greyhook had decided on three things.

First, that Dr. Calder had been fetched in the night and had remained in Mairi Bain's house longer than a man remained for ordinary fever or broken bone.

Second, that whatever had come ashore at dusk had not been another family's business long enough to remain only the Bains' by breakfast.

Third, that no one would speak plainly until someone else did first.

So the village went about its work with the careful noisiness of people determined to seem untroubled in public while listening with all they had for what might crack next.

Mairi heard it even before she rose.

The harbor always had its sounds: boots on wharf boards, pails set down harder than needed, the cry of gulls quarrelling over offal, the dull knock of a boat shifting at line. But that morning every sound carried a second meaning with it. A pause after voices outside the house. A step slowing just beyond her window. Mrs. Kincaid calling to someone farther up the lane in a tone too bright to be natural. The village was pretending not to lean toward her door.

She had not slept. Not properly.

Toward dawn Ewan had drifted at last into something like rest, not easy and not deep, but a loosening at least. Mairi had sat beside him all night in the chair with one hand on the bedcover and her head tipped back only once against the wall before the sound behind the plaster jolted her upright again.

It had come and gone in uneven intervals.

A wash. A pause. A soft inward drag. Never loud enough to be believed by anyone not trapped in the room with it. Never absent long enough to forget.

More than once she had risen and put her ear to the wall beside Ewan's bed. Each time the plaster had been cold and dry. Each time the sound ceased at once, only to return after she sat back down, as though whatever lay behind it disliked being listened to directly but did not mind being overheard.

At first light she had opened the shutter a crack and found the wall beneath the window salted faintly at the sill—a fine crust in the corners where no such thing had been the day before.

Now the room held that flat grey of morning that made every object look more tired than it was. Ewan lay turned a little toward the wall, blanket to his shoulders, hair fallen into his eyes. In daylight the shell-growth looked less otherworldly and more intolerably real. It caught the dimness in dull pale ridges at the throat and wrist, and under the blanket line she knew too well now where the seam at the shoulder lay and the branching nodes along the ribs. His mouth had relaxed in sleep. Whatever coldness lived in him had not gone, but it no longer felt like death under her hand. That was something. Not enough, but something.

Mairi rose stiffly and crossed to the kitchen.

The stove had gone low. She fed it wood, added kindling, set the kettle on, and stood a moment with both hands braced on the table while the small ordinary work of flame catching itself together steadied her.

On the table lay the doctor's thermometer where he had forgotten it in the night, or left it intentionally. Beside it sat a bowl with the last of the broth gone to skin and a rag she had used to bathe Ewan's face. The rag still smelled faintly of salt though she had rinsed it twice.

A knock came at the door.

Mairi did not turn. "If you've brought gossip, keep it and save your breath."

Mrs. Kincaid answered from the other side, "If I had gossip, I'd not bring it to the front door, would I?"

That was true enough.

Mairi went and opened to find the woman on the step with a loaf under one arm and a jar of goose fat wrapped in cloth. Mrs. Kincaid was stout, red-cheeked from weather and kitchen heat, and possessed of the peculiar village gift for making charity look like a scolding.

"You've not slept," she said at once.

"No."

"Aye, well. That shows." She pushed past before being invited, setting the loaf and jar on the table as if claiming temporary rights in the room. "I brought bread. And there's fat enough there for broth or for rubbing if the boy's chest tightens."

"He hasn't coughed."

Mrs. Kincaid's hands paused on the cloth wrapping. "No?"

"No."

The woman looked toward the back room. "Still sleeping?"

"For now."

"And the doctor?"

"Gone."

"That much the village knows."

Mairi gave her a look.

Mrs. Kincaid sniffed. "Do you think I mean to pry? If I meant to pry I'd have come before dawn and found a way to borrow salt."

"You borrowed salt last Tuesday."

"And returned better than I got." She busied herself with the kettle, peering into it though there was little to see. "You need tea in you."

"I need the house empty."

Mrs. Kincaid was quiet a beat. "Aye. I suppose you do."

That softened Mairi in spite of herself. Only slightly.

Mrs. Kincaid lowered her voice. "Did he say what it is?"

"No."

"Did he say what it isn't?"

Mairi almost laughed at that, but what came out was closer to a breath breaking wrong. "No."

The older woman turned then and studied her properly. "Well," she said after a moment, "that's a poor sort of comfort, but it's honest."

From the back room came the faint scrape of bedsheets.

Mairi was already moving before she knew she had moved. She reached the bed to find Ewan awake and watching the wall.

Not the door. Not her. The wall.

"Ewan."

His gaze shifted to her slowly, as if it had far to travel.

"How are you?"

It was a foolish question, but she asked it because mothers asked such things even when the answers were ruin.

He did not speak.

His hand lay above the blanket edge, the wrist ringed pale where the shell rose. She touched the back of his fingers. Still cool. Less stone-cold than in the night. The difference was real enough that she clung to it.

"Do you want water?"

His eyes flicked once toward the cup on the chair.

That, too, she counted.

Mairi lifted his head and held the cup to his mouth. He swallowed in small careful measures, as if each mouthful had to be negotiated first with some inward unwillingness. A little ran down his chin. She wiped it away.

Behind her, Mrs. Kincaid stood silent in the doorway with a look on her face Mairi could not bear to read.

"Take your tea," Mairi said without turning.

Mrs. Kincaid did not move.

"Go on."

"Aye."

But still she stood there one heartbeat more. Then, very quietly: "His eyes are the same."

Mairi closed hers once.

"Aye," she said.

That was nearly enough to make her weep, so she said nothing further.

When Ewan had taken what he would, she eased him back. His gaze drifted again—not to the wall this time, but to the scrap of charcoal lying on the shelf above the bed. It had been there for months with a bit of fishing twine, two smooth stones, and the broken brass hinge he had once insisted might be useful for a trap.

Mairi followed his eyes.

"You want that?"

He looked at her, then at the shelf again.

Mrs. Kincaid made a little startled sound. "He means it?"

"Yes," said Mairi. "I can see that."

She took down the charcoal and, after a brief useless hesitation over the good state of the coverlet, laid a folded bit of old wrapping paper across his knees.

"Show me, then."

Ewan's fingers closed around the charcoal awkwardly at first, as if the hand remembered the work but not the pressure. Then they steadied.

He drew a line. Stopped. Drew another crossing it at a slant. Then a curve, long and deliberate, with smaller strokes within it.

Mrs. Kincaid set down the teacup so quickly it rang against the table. "Merciful God."

"Be still," Mairi said.

She leaned closer.

It was not random scratching. Nor the distracted circles of a convalescent child. Ewan was drawing the harbor.

Not perfectly. Not with a surveyor's hand. But with enough rightness that the shape of the Mouth showed itself at once, and the inner reach, and the line of sheds, and the rise where the kirk stood. He marked the harbor entrance with two short dark notches—Crowe's Ledge and the black post, though no words named them. Then his charcoal moved outward beyond the page's natural logic, curving past where Greyhook ended into a broad sweep of open water.

There he paused.

His hand trembled once.

Mairi saw, more than heard, Mrs. Kincaid cross herself under her apron.

Then Ewan drew a circle. Not neat. Not complete at first. He went over it again until it darkened. Within it he marked a crescent shape, then a line crossing both as if to indicate a channel or cut.

The sign sat there on the page like a thing with more intention than ink.

Mairi's mouth had gone dry.

"What is that?" Mrs. Kincaid whispered.

Neither of them answered.

Ewan's hand slackened. The charcoal slipped from his fingers to the blanket.

The room went very still.

And in that stillness, from behind the wall beside the bed, came the soft unmistakable lap of water.

Mrs. Kincaid gasped aloud this time and backed into the doorframe so hard the wood knocked.

Mairi turned her head slowly toward the plaster.

The sound came again. A shallow wash. Then the faint drag as if something had receded through timber grain.

"No," Mrs. Kincaid said. "No, no."

"It's dry," Mairi said, though whether to the woman or herself she did not know. She rose and crossed to the wall, put her palm flat against it.

Cold.

Dry.

The plaster did not bulge. No damp showed through. And yet under her hand she fancied she felt—not movement exactly, but a depth that did not belong there, as if the house had gained an interior it had not possessed yesterday.

She snatched her hand away.

Behind her Ewan made a small sound.

Mairi wheeled.

It was not speech. Barely even voice. But it was the first sound from him that was not breath, not swallowing, not the accidental noise of a body. A low rough catch in the throat, almost pain and almost warning.

She went to him at once. "What is it?"

His eyes were wide now. Not with fright. With listening.

He lifted one hand and pointed—not at the wall, but downward.

To the floor.

Mrs. Kincaid said, “I’m away.”

Mairi barely heard her.

She dropped to one knee and looked under the bed.

Dark boards. Dust. A single lost button near the back leg. Nothing else.

Then she saw the line.

Along the seam where floor met wall there had formed, fine as frost and just as white, a scattering of salt crystals. Not many. A tracing. A patient bright edge running six inches one way, four the other, vanishing beneath the bedframe.

Mrs. Kincaid had come close enough to see it before courage failed her entirely.

“That was not there.”

“No.”

“Not there this morning.”

Mairi did not answer.

Mrs. Kincaid backed out into the kitchen. “I’ll fetch—” She stopped. “I don’t know who I’ll fetch.”

Old Ailie, Mairi thought at once, and hated herself for thinking it.

"No one yet," she said. "If the village hears before I tell it, I'll have six women praying in the lane and three men offering to tear down my wall."

"And wouldn't you let them?"

"No."

Mrs. Kincaid stared at the salt, then at Ewan, then at Mairi. "You're alone too much in this."

"Yes."

The woman swallowed. "I'll stay anyway."

Mairi looked at her then, really looked, and saw the fear plainly. Mrs. Kincaid was not staying because she was unafraid. She was staying because she had known Mairi since girlhood, had washed Ewan when he was born, had carried soup after the drowning, and had the sort of practical loyalty that made cowards out of no one but required bravery from no one in advance either.

Mairi said, "Make more tea, then."

Mrs. Kincaid nodded too quickly. "Aye."

By midday Dr. Calder returned with his own horse and a face set against curiosity.

He barely removed his coat before asking, "Any change?"

Mairi handed him the paper.

He took it, frowned, then frowned harder.

"Did he draw this?"

"You see anyone else in the bed?"

Calder ignored that. He held the paper to the window light. "This is the harbor."

"Yes."

"And this?"

Ewan, watching from the bed, touched one finger to the symbol at the page's edge.

Calder glanced from the mark to the child. Something sharpened behind his eyes—not excitement exactly, but the dangerous near-cousin to it that physicians, scholars, and fools all mistake for usefulness.

He crossed to the bed and crouched.

"Can you make more of it?"

Ewan looked at him, then away.

"Do you know where this is?"

Nothing.

Calder tried a different tack. "Is it a rock? A shoal?"

At the word *shoal*, Ewan's eyes snapped toward the window.

All three adults saw it.

Calder rose slowly. "Well."

Mrs. Kincaid, who had not left after all and was now peeling potatoes with more force than needed, said, "Don't say it like you've found a penny in the road."

Calder gave her the briefest glance. "Would you prefer I say nothing?"

"I'd prefer you knew whether silence was safer."

Mairi almost liked her for that.

Calder set the paper on the table and went to the wall. "Where?"

"There." Mairi indicated the place beside the bed.

"And the floor." Mrs. Kincaid pointed with the knife, then reconsidered and lowered it quickly.

He bent to inspect the salt at the seam. He touched one finger to it, rubbed thumb and forefinger together, sniffed, then, to Mairi's disgust, tasted the barest grain.

"It's salt," he said.

"How reassuring," said Mrs. Kincaid.

Calder ignored her. He inspected the plaster, tapped it, pressed his ear against it. The wall gave him only ordinary house-sounds while he listened. When he drew back, expression sharpening in irritation, the soft water-lap resumed almost at once.

Mairi watched his face as he heard it. It was a mean satisfaction, but she took it.

"There," she said.

He did not pretend this time. "Aye."

"What is it?"

"I don't know."

"And if you cut the wall open?"

"No."

All three of them turned.

Old Ailie Crowe stood in the doorway, shawl wrapped tight, as if summoned by the sentence itself.

Mairi said, "Who asked you in?"

Ailie's eyes went to the paper on the table, the wall, the bed, and finally Ewan. "No one. That is why I came."

Calder straightened. "Mrs. Crowe, I have not said I mean to cut the wall."

"You were thinking it."

He did not answer, which was answer enough.

Ailie crossed to the table and looked down at the drawing. Her lined face changed less than other people's did, but Mairi saw the life in it draw taut.

"That mark," Ailie said quietly.

"You know it?" Mairi asked.

Ailie's gaze stayed on the paper. "I know I've seen its like."

"Where?"

"Not in a place I'd care to say before supper."

Mairi's temper flared sharp and clean. "Then say it now and spare the meal."

Ailie looked up. "In old wood."

The room held still.

"What old wood?" said Calder.

"The sort under newer names."

"That means nothing."

"It means enough."

Mairi stepped closer. "Say it plain."

Ailie nodded once toward the back wall. "There's timber in this house that was not first cut for this house."

Mairi almost dismissed it at once. Every house in Greyhook had timber reused from somewhere. Boats broke, sheds collapsed, storms gave what storms gave, and no one on this coast was proud enough to let sound wood rot for want of a first purpose.

But Ailie went on.

"Years ago, before your mother came to this house, there was another place here or near enough to here. Part of it came down in one winter storm, part was taken later for repair timber. The old men said some of the back beams had been salvaged before that from the shore road—older yet. Not village-cut. Drifted or broken from something else."

"From what else?" said Calder.

Ailie shrugged once. "If they knew, they didn't say it to me."

Mrs. Kincaid said, "Everyone reuses timber."

"Not all timber takes the same kind of memory," Ailie said.

Calder gave a short dry laugh. "Memory."

Ailie turned to him. "You have a better word?"

"No."

"Then leave off mocking the one in reach."

Mairi was watching Ewan. At the mention of the older timber, his face had altered again in that faint, terrible way it did when something struck true. His eyes had gone to the wall, and his hand, still weak, moved once over the blanket as if tracing a line she could not see.

She took up the paper and laid it before him again. "Show me."

His fingers found the charcoal more quickly this time.

He drew not the harbor now but a simple set of lines: one horizontal, two vertical, another crossing above them. It might have been nothing. It might have been the frame of a shed or a child's first house-shape.

Then he added smaller marks beneath. Short parallel strokes.

Pilings, Mairi thought at once, though she did not know why.

Ewan moved the charcoal to the side and made the circle-and-crescent sign again. This time he placed it beyond the upright strokes, then drew a line from one to the other.

Ailie shut her eyes briefly.

"What is it?" Mairi said.

The old woman opened them. "A way."

"To where?"

Ailie looked at her son. "Not where. Through."

Calder said, "That is nonsense."

"Is it?" said Ailie, and indicated the wall, the salt, the child in the bed. "You've seen more nonsense in this room by noon than most men do in a lifetime."

Calder's mouth closed.

Mairi set the paper down carefully. She no longer trusted quick motions.

"What do I do?"

No one answered at once.

Outside, the village moved on with its ordinary noon life: a hammer striking somewhere by the sheds, a horse blowing in harness, a woman calling for her youngest to come in and wash. All of it so stubbornly ordinary that for one instant Mairi hated every sound.

Then the wall behind the bed gave a long low wash, not loud but so unmistakable that no one could pretend this time.

Ewan flinched.

That decided her more surely than any explanation might have.

She turned to Calder. "No knives."

He blinked. "I did not—"

"No knives. No scraping. No taking samples. No cutting him and no opening that wall."

His eyes narrowed. "Mrs. Bain, if this is structural—"

"If this is structural, then it has waited years to choose its hour, and I'll not have half Greyhook ripping boards apart over my son's head."

Ailie said quietly, "She's right in that much."

Calder looked from one woman to the other and recognized, perhaps, that the room had gone from his keeping entirely.

"What, then?" he asked. "We sit and listen to a wall?"

Mairi answered before anyone else could.

"We watch."

He drew breath to argue, then let it go. "Very well. But if the condition worsens—"

"I'll send."

He collected his bag with more abruptness than dignity. At the door he paused, looking back once at Ewan, once at the drawing on the table. "Do not speak that word near him again."

"What word?" Mrs. Kincaid asked.

Calder's gaze moved to the symbol dark on the page.

"Shoal," he said.

When he had gone, taking his uncertainty with him only to spread it elsewhere, the house seemed no quieter for his absence.

Ailie moved to the wall and laid her knuckles against it, not rapping, merely touching.

"Old timber," she murmured.

Mairi had grown tired of the phrase. "You've said that twice as if saying it a third will teach it to me."

Ailie looked over her shoulder. "Then hear the rest. If this wall carries the wrong wood, the sound may not be coming through from outside."

Mairi felt the kitchen tilt very slightly around her.

"Then from where?"

Ailie gave no answer.

Mrs. Kincaid, for once, had none either.

Ewan did.

Only not in words.

He lifted the charcoal once more and, with an effort that made his hand shake, drew a single line beneath the little upright strokes.

Then another below that. Then another.

Depth marks.

Mairi knew them without knowing how she knew.

Below the timber, below the house, below the village itself, he was drawing down.

That afternoon the wind rose and the sea at the harbor mouth went the color of old iron.

And in Mairi Bain's back room, behind the dry plaster beside her son's bed, the tide went on coming in.

4

The Ledger Without Pages

By afternoon the whole village knew Mairi Bain had barred her back room against advice, pity, and common sense alike.

What they did not know, because she had not let them see it, was the paper on the kitchen table with Ewan's black marks darkening toward the edge like a route no one living had asked him to learn.

She had folded it twice and slid it beneath the bread board after Dr. Calder left. Not because she thought the thing safer hidden, but because she could not bear every eye in Greyhook passing over it and pretending to ignorance afterward.

The wind freshened through the day. By three o'clock the harbor had taken on that leaden, hard-creased look that meant no one with wit enough to grow old would choose open water unless pressed by debt or stupidity. Men worked close to shore. Nets were checked, not cast. A pair of boys were sent to bring in the smaller skiff from the north side before the weather worsened. Doors latched harder than usual. Smoke from the chimneys streamed low and bent.

Inside Mairi's house, the tide in the wall kept its own hour.

It did not sound constantly now. Instead it came in intervals—long quiets stretched so thin she nearly convinced herself she had imagined it all, followed by a soft inward wash from behind the bed, or a low shifting drag beneath the floor seam that raised the small hairs along her wrists before her ears caught it. Each time it came, Ewan's eyes would lift, not startled but attentive, and fix somewhere just beyond the plaster as if he were listening to instructions she could not hear.

By midafternoon he had drawn no more.

He took broth in six swallows and no more. Water in four. Spoke not at all.

But when Mairi asked him simple things—are you cold, does your side hurt, do you want the blanket higher—she had the beginning of answers now. A blink. A motion of the hand. The slow turn of his eyes. Not enough to be called recovery. Enough to feel like someone still lived inside the silence.

Mrs. Kincaid stayed until the light began to fail, then rose with all the reluctance of a woman who has decided on decency and resents being made to practice it so long.

"I've my own stove to tend."

"Yes."

"I'll send over soup."

"You've sent enough."

"That's not for you to measure."

Mairi almost smiled at that. Almost.

At the door, Mrs. Kincaid hesitated. "Will you have someone sit tonight?"

"No."

"Mairi."

"No."

The older woman shifted her shawl tighter under her chin. "Then I'll come in the morning whether wanted or not."

"That has never stopped you yet."

Mrs. Kincaid gave the briefest huff and went out into the lane, closing the door firmly behind her against wind and watching ears alike.

Old Ailie Crowe had not left.

She sat at the table with her hands wrapped around a teacup gone cold long since, as if she had been carved into the place by weather and obstinacy both. Mairi had tried twice to put her out. Twice Ailie had answered with something so maddeningly unhurried that no proper quarrel could get hold of it.

Now Mairi stood at the stove, scraping the bottom of the broth pot with more force than was necessary, and said,

"If you've no more to say than old timber, you may go warm your own walls."

Ailie looked toward the back room without turning her head. "Mine are not the walls speaking."

"Yours have likely more reason to."

"Likely."

Mairi set the spoon down. "You enjoy this."

"No."

"You talk as if you do."

Ailie's face shifted then, not much, only enough to let Mairi see the oldness in her more clearly. Not age alone. Use. History. The look of someone who has spent years learning how little comfort truth brings when it finally puts on shoes and walks into a room.

"I enjoy being late less than I would enjoy being too early," she said.

Mairi had no answer ready for that, which irritated her more than if she had been mocked outright.

Instead she said, "You've seen the mark before."

Ailie was silent a moment.

"Yes."

"Where?"

"In a ledger first."

"What ledger?"

"Then in wood. Then nowhere I could admit it."

Mairi stared at her. "That is not an answer."

"It is what you've got."

Mairi took one step toward the table. "If you mean to play at this, do it elsewhere."

Ailie met her eyes at last. "The old kirk chest."

The words landed cleanly.

Mairi drew in breath.

"The records?"

"Some of them."

"You said a ledger."

Ailie nodded. "I said true."

The old kirk chest stood in the vestry room of the church on the rise, where parish notes, family entries, weather accounts, and a hundred little scraps of local fact had been kept under lock across years of damp, ministerial order, and selective memory. Mairi had gone there once already, before Ewan returned, to search drowning lists and harbor losses after the accident. She had found scraped pages and euphemisms instead of answers.

She said, "You saw the mark there when?"

"Years ago."

"Why were you looking?"

Ailie's mouth thinned. "Because there was another child once."

The broth spoon slipped from Mairi's hand and rang against the iron stove plate.

Ailie did not move.

"What child?"

"Not returned."

"Then what has that to do with my son?"

"It began with a sound in a pantry wall," Ailie said quietly.

The room changed shape around Mairi.

Not physically. Not by any outward shift. But all at once the last day and night seemed to deepen beneath her feet and reveal older boards underneath.

"Whose child?" she asked.

Ailie's gaze dropped to the cold tea. "A Crowe child."

The answer explained much and nothing.

"Yours?"

"No." A pause. "My sister's girl."

Mairi pulled out the chair opposite and sat before her knees failed the effort. "Tell it plain."

Ailie considered, as if deciding whether plainness had yet earned its keep.

"She was seven. Heard singing, they said, from behind the pantry wall. Not music. Not proper singing. More the shape of it. She'd stand with her ear pressed there till the bread spoiled in her hand. Then one morning she was gone."

"How long ago?"

"Twenty years and more."

"Gone how?"

Ailie's eyes lifted, sharp despite the wear in them. "If we'd known how, the knowing would have done us more good."

Mairi swallowed against the dryness in her throat. "And in the ledger?"

"The minister then kept notes not fit for the pulpit. Odd bits. House complaints. Things to be dismissed in daylight and written down in private all the same." Ailie tapped one finger on the tabletop. "There was a sign drawn in the margin. Yours."

"Our mark?"

"Your son's mark."

Mairi thought of the folded paper beneath the bread board and felt all at once as though it burned there through wood and cloth alike.

"What did it mean?"

Ailie gave the only honest answer possible and therefore the most useless. "I don't know."

"Then what good are you?"

The words came harsher than Mairi intended.

Ailie absorbed them without flinch. "Little enough, usually."

For a moment neither spoke.

Then from the back room came the low wash of water behind the wall.

Both women turned.

It lasted longer this time. Not loud. Not threatening. Merely present, with the obscene confidence of a sound that knew itself tolerated.

Mairi rose. Ailie rose more slowly. They crossed the room together.

Ewan was awake. He had pushed himself halfway upright against the pillow with more strength than he had shown since the shore, and his eyes were fixed not on the wall now but on the little window beside the bed.

Beyond the glass, dusk was settling over Greyhook in layers of iron-grey and blue-black. The harbor itself could not be seen from this angle, only the lane, the lower corner of the Kincaids' roof, and a strip of darkening sky.

But Ewan was not looking at the lane.

He was looking through it all, as if distance had ceased to behave for him in the usual way.

Mairi sat on the bed's edge at once. "What is it?"

He lifted one hand and touched two fingers to the glass.

Then drew them downward slowly.

A line.

Not on the pane itself. In the air. In meaning.

Ailie said behind her, "He's showing soundings again."

Mairi looked back sharply. "Again?"

But Ailie was watching Ewan with that same old measuring attention.

"He's not drawing a map alone," she said. "He's drawing depth."

Mairi turned back to her son. "Depth to what?"

Ewan's mouth opened.

Nothing.

Then his face tightened with sudden effort and the fingers at the window curled hard enough that his nails clicked softly against the glass.

From somewhere outside came the sound of the church bell.

One strike only.

Then, after a pause too long to be ordinary—

a second.

Mairi froze.

The bell was not meant to be rung after evening unless for death, fire, or wreck. And no child in Greyhook would dare pull that rope for mischief now, not with the village already breathing shallow over the Bains' house.

The second strike hung in the wind.

Ailie said, "That'll be him."

"Who?"

"The Reverend."

Mairi did not ask how she knew. Some knowledge in villages moved faster than feet.

Sure enough, not long after, boots sounded on the lane and a brisk, disciplined knock came at the front door: not the hesitant rap of a neighbor bringing broth, nor the blunt demand of Tam, but the measured knock of a man who believed doors should understand themselves.

Mairi stood. "Stay."

Whether she meant it to Ewan or Ailie was unclear even to herself.

At the door she found Reverend Iain Sutherland in his dark coat, wind-reddened at the cheeks, hat in one hand. He was a spare man, not tall, with a narrow face sharpened further by restraint. His hair, what remained of it, had gone mostly silver above the ears. He had the grave, watchful look of someone long practiced in hearing the worst before supper and being expected to improve it by the time grace was said.

"Mrs. Bain."

"Reverend."

He glanced past her shoulder into the dim kitchen. "May I come in?"

Mairi considered saying no.

That she considered it at all told her how much had altered in one day.

Still, there were refusals a woman could make in Greyhook and refusals that only fed the village harder. So she stepped aside.

He entered, removed his hat fully, and stood a moment in the kitchen as if listening. Not piously. Practically. Mairi noticed that and disliked him less for it.

"I've had calls," he said.

"You always do."

"Yes."

The answer was so dry that, under other circumstances, she might have appreciated it.

His eyes moved to Ailie Crowe, standing in the back-room doorway like some weathered post the house had grown around.

"Mrs. Crowe."

"Reverend."

"I see we are well attended."

Ailie said, "No one's well attended in this house."

He inclined his head the smallest degree, conceding either the point or the rudeness.

Then his gaze shifted to the bed.

It was slight. It was immediate. A tightening around the eyes, nothing more. But Mairi saw it. So did Ailie. The minister had expected something troublesome, perhaps alarming, perhaps even grotesque by the village's hungry telling.

He had not expected Ewan Bain.

Not truly.

Ewan was propped against the pillow, blanket to the chest, hair fallen dark across the brow. At first glance in the low room he might have been any sick child returned from weather, all hollows and silence. It took a second look to see the shell at the throat. Another to recognize the stillness in him that was not simple fatigue.

"Ewan," the Reverend said.

Ewan's eyes moved to him.

No answer.

The minister stepped no nearer. “I heard you had come home.”

Mairi said, “So had the whole coast by noon, I expect.”

A pause.

Then Sutherland turned to her with more gentleness than she wanted and more sense than she had expected. “Mrs. Bain, I did not come to question what your house has not had time to understand.”

“Then why come?”

“To see. To hear what is needed. To prevent the village from becoming worse company than it already is.”

Ailie gave a short sound that might have been approval.

Mairi folded her arms. “And can you?”

“No.”

That nearly won him another measure of her patience.

He looked again to the bed, and this time his eye caught the folded paper on the chair—Mairi had brought it from under the bread board without knowing she had done so when the bell sounded, wanting it near.

“What is that?”

“Nothing for the kirk chest,” Ailie said.

Mairi shot her a warning glance, then picked up the paper herself and held it closed.

Sutherland, seeing enough to understand refusal was in the room with him already, let the matter drop for the moment. “Dr. Calder has been?”

“Yes.”

“And?”

“He knows as much as the rest of us.”

“Which is?”

“Nothing useful.”

The Reverend accepted that, though his eyes told her he did not believe the word *nothing*.

Before he could ask more, the wall behind the bed gave its sound again.

Soft. Patient. A little inward pull followed by the faint lap of receding water.

The minister’s head turned very slightly.

He did not start. He did not pray. He did not pretend he had heard only settling wood.

For that alone Mairi felt a flicker of respect.

Ailie said, “There now.”

Sutherland stood perfectly still until the sound faded.

Then: “How often?”

“Enough,” Mairi said.

“Since when?”

“Last night.”

“And before?”

“No.”

The minister's eyes went to the back wall, to the bed's position against it, then down to the floor seam where a few grains of salt still held bright in the failing light.

He stepped nearer and crouched. Touched one finger to the white trace. Rubbed it between thumb and forefinger. Said nothing.

At last he rose.

"There are older entries," he said.

Mairi stared at him. "You know that, do you?"

Ailie's mouth pressed thin with something almost like satisfaction.

Sutherland did not look at her. "I know the kirk books are not complete."

"That is a gentle word for it."

"It is the word I am using."

Mairi took one breath, then another. "I went to the chest after the accident."

"Yes."

"You knew that too?"

"I was told you asked for burial entries and weather losses."

"And I found pages missing."

He did not deny it.

Mairi said, "Mrs. Crowe says there was a mark in one of the older ledgers."

Sutherland's eyes moved at last to Ailie. "Did she."

"She did."

A long second passed.

Then the minister said, “There may have been.”

“May?”

“I have seen notes not preserved in the formal books.”

That phrase struck Mairi like a slap. “Not preserved.”

“It is possible—”

“No. Say it plain as she won’t. Were they removed?”

Sutherland held her gaze. “Some were set aside.”

“By whom?”

“Men before me.”

“For what reason?”

No answer came quickly. At last: “To keep disorder from taking root in ignorance.”

Ailie gave a low, disgusted laugh.

Mairi’s anger sharpened so fast it steadied her. “And did it work?”

The Reverend did not answer that either.

Good, she thought. Let him stand in his own failure.

She unfolded the paper and held it out.

The minister looked down at Ewan’s marks.

His face changed less than most men’s did, but enough. The sign within the circle had struck him cleanly.

“You have seen it,” Mairi said.

Not a question.

After a moment, he nodded.

“Where?”

"In the margin of a private account-book kept by Mr. Calder's grandfather."

"Hugh Calder's?"

"Yes."

The old schoolmaster-reader, then, not the doctor. Another Calder. Another man with ink and worry and the bad habit of writing down what daylight could not use.

Mairi said, "And what did he call it?"

Sutherland hesitated too long.

Ailie answered for him.

"Not a place," she said. "A hinge."

The room went colder without any change in the stove.

Mairi looked from one old face to the other. "You both knew that and said nothing?"

Sutherland's voice came grave and dry. "Mrs. Bain, there is a difference between knowing a word and trusting what men have made of it."

"Then trust my son's hand over theirs."

That landed.

The Reverend looked again at Ewan, who was watching him now with a steadiness neither childlike nor inhuman but somehow both at once. Then Sutherland looked back to the mark on the page.

"At the kirk," he said slowly, "there are loose papers in a side chest not usually handled. Weather notes. House complaints. Burial matters not entered publicly. I have not read them all."

"Why not?"

"Because ministers, like doctors, are too often called to what is immediate and too little to what is old."

Ailie said, "That and cowardice."

He did not object.

Mairi folded the paper once, sharply. "Then you'll read them tonight."

The wind struck the house hard then, rattling the shutter in its catch. Ewan flinched, but not at the wind. His eyes went again to the wall.

The tide-sound came, stronger than before.

This time it did not stop at a single wash. It continued in three slow breaths, with a depth in it that made the room seem to tilt very slightly toward the bed, as if all the old timber in the house had remembered some older burden and were leaning to hear.

Sutherland went pale.

Only a little. Enough.

He said, "No one moves the bed."

Ailie's eyes narrowed. "You know that too?"

"I know enough not to be a fool before women who've less excuse for it."

Mairi almost smiled at that and hated the impulse.

"Then we are done speaking," she said. "You'll go to the kirk. You'll bring what there is. And if you think to spare me any part of it because I am tired or a woman or a mother, you'll save yourself the trouble."

The Reverend inclined his head once.

"I will bring what is there."

He put on his hat, then paused at the door. "Keep no one else in the room with him tonight unless they are wanted."

Mairi frowned. "Why?"

He looked back toward the bed, toward the wall, toward the salt at the seam.

"Because houses sometimes learn a thing by repetition."

Ailie muttered, "Aye."

The minister went out into the rising dark.

For a long moment after the door shut, Mairi stood still with the folded paper in her hand and the sound of the wall breathing behind her son.

Then she turned to Ailie.

"You knew he'd come to that."

"I hoped."

Mairi gave one short, incredulous laugh. "You play old games with everyone."

"No," Ailie said, and for once there was no riddling in it. "Only with those who still think the straight road is the safest."

From the bed came the scratch of movement.

Ewan had taken up the charcoal again.

Mairi crossed at once, Ailie behind her slower but no less intent.

On the paper's lower edge, beneath the sign, beneath the upright marks and depth lines, Ewan had added something new.

A narrow dark stroke. Then another crossing it. Then a row of smaller vertical marks.

Not pilings this time.

Stones.

No—not stones.

Graves.

Mairi felt the blood leave her face.

Ailie whispered, "Church ground."

And behind the plaster, as if in answer, the tide came in once more.

5

Rooms That Take the Tide

That night Mairi did not light the second lamp.

One was enough for work. One was enough for watching. Two would only have made the room look fuller than it was, and she had no wish to give the house more shape than it already possessed.

The weather worsened after dark. Not into storm, not yet, but into the kind of wind that made all things provisional. It came in long damp pushes from the east and laid itself against the village with patient force. The shutter gave now and then in its catch. Somewhere beyond the lane a loose board knocked in a slow uneven rhythm. From the harbor came the familiar night sounds—rope strain, a piling's complaint, a boat answering tide with its hull—but all of them seemed farther off than they should have been, as though the house had drawn a little away from the rest of Greyhook and was listening elsewhere.

Mairi sat by Ewan's bed with the folded paper in her lap.

He had not drawn again since the graves.

At least, she had taken them for graves. She could not see what else they might have been—those small upright strokes in a row beneath the sign and beneath the soundings, set just so, like markers in a place where the ground had already been measured by sorrow. Church ground, Ailie had said.

Mairi had folded the paper sharply then and put it away before Ewan could add more. She was not sure whether she meant to keep the drawings from the room, or the room from the drawings.

Ailie Crowe had gone at last only because the Reverend was expected back from the kirk and Mairi insisted she would not have the whole village's oldest worries stacked in one kitchen like winter wood. Ailie had wrapped her shawl about herself and stood at the threshold with the expression of a woman leaving a stove untended in a windy house.

"If he brings papers," she had said, "read the margin as close as the text."

"As if I can know one from the other."

"You'll know."

Then she had gone up the lane into the dark without a lantern.

Now Mairi listened to the house and waited for the minister.

Ewan lay turned a little toward the wall again, not sleeping but nearly still enough to counterfeit it. His breathing—or what stood in for it now—had settled into that troubling rhythm she had come to dread: slow, shallow, then with the faintest pause as if some inward part of him listened before continuing. She had watched his chest long enough to know it no longer rose quite like an ordinary child's. Not much differently. Not enough to see unless one knew him. But mothers knew the millimeter shifts by which life betrayed itself.

She reached and drew the blanket a little higher.

At her touch, Ewan's eyes opened.

"I did not wake you," she said.

He looked at her, then past her toward the kitchen, then back to the wall.

"You hear it again?"

A blink.

Yes, then.

The tide had been quieter since dusk. Less frequent, but deeper when it came. The sound no longer resembled a mere wash behind plaster. It had gathered weight. Not loudness—weight. As if what moved beyond the wall did so through more than one thickness of matter now.

Mairi rose and crossed the room, lamp in hand.

The wall showed nothing new.

The paper was faded as ever, the crack near the window no wider, the sill only lightly crusted where salt had bloomed there before. She crouched and held the lamp lower along the floor seam. The earlier white trace had spread. Not dramatically. Not enough for any ordinary eye to cry flood or seep. But the salt now ran under the bed farther than before and curled along the edge of the skirting in a line too deliberate to be accidental.

She set down the lamp and touched the boards.

Dry.

Cold.

No give beneath her fingers. No hidden wet in the grain.

Behind her Ewan made that low rough throat-catch again—the almost-voice that had become warning.

Mairi turned at once.

"What is it?"

His eyes were not on the wall now.

They were on the room itself.

She followed his gaze and saw nothing at first beyond the familiar objects made strange by lamplight: the blanket box, the peg with his Sunday jacket hanging unused since August, the shelf leaning still where Tam had fixed it badly, the chair she had worn her spine against for two nights. Then the lamplight shifted as the flame drew long in the draft, and Mairi saw that the shells along Ewan's wrist were reflecting not yellow but a dim colder gleam from somewhere below the level of the lamp.

She looked down.

At the base of the far wall opposite the bed, just where kitchen met back room through the narrow doorframe, a second salt line had appeared.

Not from the same seam. Not connected to the first.

A separate pale tracing, low and new.

Mairi stood very still.

The room wants barring, Ailie had said.

Not the wall. The room.

The thought entered Mairi cleanly and made no sense she wanted.

Then the tide-sound came.

Not behind the bed this time.

Across the room.

A soft inward wash from the opposite wall, followed by the same patient drag she had begun to know too well.

The house had taken a second breath.

"No," she said aloud.

But the room did not care what she denied.

A knock came at the front door.

Mairi nearly laughed from the abruptness of the ordinary intrusion. She took up the lamp and went through the kitchen, every board too loud under her feet, and opened to Reverend Sutherland with wind at his back and a leather satchel under one arm.

He looked at her face once and said, "It has worsened."

"Yes."

He entered without waiting for permission this time, which was just as well, for she was in no condition to produce it.

He set the satchel on the table, removed his coat, and from the bag drew a tied bundle of papers, a thin ledger, and a smaller wrapped packet that might once have been orderly but had since suffered years of damp and storage. The smell that rose from them was old paper, mildew, and that peculiar stale sweetness of records too long shut away from air and yet not long enough from hands.

"There was more than I thought," he said.

"You have read them?"

"Enough."

"That means no."

"It means not all."

She wanted to strike him.

Instead she took the ledger and opened it under the lamp.

The writing inside was cramped and old-fashioned, the ink browned, the hand of a man who mistrusted waste in line as in life. Several pages had been cut away cleanly. Others were crossed through. In the margins lay notes of weather, burial entries, repairs to the church chest, one record of a pew dispute so petty Mairi could have admired it under other conditions.

Then she found it.

Not text. A drawing.

No more than a sign in the margin beside a paragraph scored half through: a darkened circle, a crescent within it, and a line crossing both at a slant.

Mairi sat down.

Sutherland remained standing. "That is not the earliest occurrence."

"There are earlier?"

He slid the loose packet toward her.

The first pages were not pages at all but folded scraps—weather notes, names, household complaints, all in different hands. One, written in a thinner earlier script, bore the heading:

Concerning certain complaints from the lower houses upon nights of turn-tide.

Below followed a list.

Hearing of wash within dry timbers. Salt appearing at bed-boards. A child given to standing at the north wall and saying there was room beyond it. A mark found drawn with coal beside the pantry shelf, likeness uncertain.

Beside that final line, in a later hand, was written: **same sign as in Calder notes.**

Mairi looked up sharply. "Calder."

"The schoolmaster-reader," said Sutherland. "Hugh's grandfather."

"Ailie said the mark was in his account-book."

"It is." He touched the thin ledger. "This copy is excerpted from that."

Excerpted.

A church word for theft, Mairi thought bitterly.

"Read," she said.

Sutherland hesitated. "Some of this is second-hand, or worse."

"Read."

He took the book from her, turned pages with careful fingers, and found the place he wanted. When he began, his voice altered—not sermon voice, not pastoral comfort, but that plain restrained cadence ministers used when unwilling to lend themselves too fully to another man's error.

"'The sign recurring in the lower settlement is not, I think, to be accounted for by childish imitation alone, as it appears in households too distant for such exchange and is in one case found marked in salt rather than coal.'"

He stopped.

"In salt?" Mairi said.

Sutherland nodded once and continued.

"'The old woman Crowe reports hearing from her mother that certain shore-people before the kirk families called it not a mark but a meeting of ways, though whether this be Popish relic, heathen usage, or common coastal fancy I do not determine.'"

A wind-gust pushed at the shutter.

Then, from the back room, came the double sound of the house breathing in two places at once.

The minister stopped reading.

Mairi said, “You hear it.”

“Yes.”

“Then leave off caution.”

Sutherland closed the ledger over one finger. “Mrs. Bain, what I have are scraps. Fragments men kept because they did not know whether to destroy them.”

“Meaning they wanted them near.”

“Meaning they feared the use others might make.”

“Of what use?” Mairi said. “No one in this house is seeking a prayer-book charm against mildew.”

The minister’s eyes went to the back room. “No,” he said quietly. “They feared invitation.”

The word dropped heavily.

Mairi turned it over in her mind and hated what shape it made beside Ewan’s drawings.

“Read the rest.”

Sutherland opened farther on.

“‘There is old report among the fishing families that some dwellings are more apt to take the tide than others, especially where back timbers were not first-cut for Christian use. In such houses, after severe weather, one must be careful what grief is spoken aloud and toward what wall.’”

Mairi laughed once. It was not amusement.

"Toward what wall."

"I did not write it."

"No. Men before you only kept it hidden."

He said nothing.

The tide-sound came again, nearer.

Not louder. Nearer.

It now seemed to travel not behind the back-room plaster but through the threshold between kitchen and bedchamber, as if the two rooms had become adjoining spaces to something else and the house had not yet decided which side of itself to belong to.

Sutherland closed the ledger completely. "Show me."

Mairi took the lamp and led him.

Ewan had not moved much. He lay still with his eyes open and the blanket high. But his face had tightened, and his left hand gripped the coverlet hard enough that the shell-ridged wrist stood out pale and severe above the wool.

The Reverend halted just inside the room.

His gaze went first to the original wall by the bed. Then to the opposite wall where the second line of salt had formed. Then to the floor between.

"What?" Mairi demanded.

He crouched and held the lamp low.

The salt lines did not stop where she had thought they stopped. In the right light they showed themselves as only the visible edges of something fainter—traces extending in a thin broken curve from one side of the room to the other, interrupted by board gaps, table legs, bed shadows.

A shape.

Not random spread. Not ordinary seep.

A broad arc, as though the room were being inscribed from within.

Sutherland said, very softly, "It's mapping the space."

Mairi stared at him. "What is?"

He did not answer.

Ewan did.

Not in speech. In action.

He released the blanket, reached toward the shelf with unmistakable effort, and opened and closed his fingers once.

"Charcoal," Mairi said.

She fetched it, along with the paper, and laid both before him.

His hand shook worse than before. Twice he failed to grip the charcoal properly. Mairi nearly stopped him. Then his fingers found the hold and steadied.

He drew the room.

Not the harbor this time.

The room.

Roughly, but clear enough: bed, window, door, opposite wall. Then he marked one arc from the wall by the bed, and another from the far wall, curving inward.

Meeting.

A hinge.

Beneath the crossing point he drew the same circle-crescent mark.

Then, below that, one short row of upright strokes.

Again the graves.

Mairi felt her own breath shorten.

Sutherland said, "Church ground."

"Yes," she said. "We had that much before you brought a satchel to repeat it."

He did not rebuke her. He was staring at the drawing the way a man stares at a shoreline that has just been recognized as the wrong coast.

Then Ewan added something new.

A box-shape. Narrow. Rectangular. Set beside the row of strokes.

The minister made a sound under his breath.

"What?"

He looked up at her slowly. "A chest."

The kirk chest.

Mairi turned that over once and found no comfort in it.

"You think he means the papers?"

"I think he means a place in the church ground or under it where something was kept."

Ailie's voice came from the kitchen doorway.

"Or moved."

Neither had heard her enter.

She stood there with rain beginning to silver her shawl and a lantern in one hand, as though she had left and reconsidered both weather and conscience before reaching her own gate.

Mairi said, not kindly, "Does no one in Greyhook respect a closed door?"

"No one tonight," Ailie said.

She came in, saw the salt pattern, the drawing, the minister's open ledger, and gave one curt nod as if several private suspicions had just been promoted to public office.

"You found it, then."

Sutherland said, "Not all."

"No," said Ailie. "Only enough."

Mairi rounded on both of them. "Enough for what?"

Ailie set down the lantern. "Enough to know your room's not haunting. It's joining."

The word struck harder than invitation had.

Joining.

Mairi looked from the salt arc on the floor to the dark sign on the page, and for the first time she understood why Ewan's room had changed from a place being troubled into a place being used.

The walls were not being attacked.

They were being aligned.

"No," she said again, but weaker now.

Ailie did not argue with the denial. "There were houses before this one," she said. "And before those, something nearer the shore-road. When old places come down in Greyhook, folk take what can be used and build on. Wood, hinges, pegs, nails if they're worth drawing. If the wrong things were taken apart and spread through the village, then maybe what was once kept in one place has been trying years to remember itself through many."

Sutherland said, "That is speculation."

"Aye," Ailie said. "And still better than your predecessors' habit of cutting pages out."

The minister had the decency to go quiet.

Mairi sat on the edge of the bed because the room had gone too large to stand in.

"What joins to what?"

No one answered at once.

Then Ewan, with painful effort, turned his face not to the wall, not to the floor, but toward the church on the rise beyond sight of the house.

His mouth opened.

His throat worked visibly. Once. Twice.

And then, in a voice so rough and low it hardly seemed made by a child, he said one word.

"Below."

Silence followed it.

Not ordinary silence. The sort that falls after a thing too long feared has at last chosen language.

Mairi's whole body tightened. She took his shoulders lightly, too lightly, afraid of where skin became shell beneath the blanket.

"Below what?"

His eyes slipped shut.

No answer came.

Only the tide, moving now through both walls of the room in slow patient breaths, as if what lay beneath Greyhook had heard itself spoken of and was pleased to be acknowledged.

6

What the Boatmen Agreed to Say

By morning the word *below* had done what words always did in Greyhook once heard by more than one soul: it had altered shape before breakfast and set half the village to carrying versions of it up and down the lanes under cover of ordinary business.

No one came to Mairi's door and said, *Your boy spoke in the night and named what lies under us.*

Instead: Mrs. Kincaid arrived with oatcakes and did not ask whether Ewan had spoken, only whether his throat pained him. A boy sent from the Reids came wanting to borrow a hammer no one in the Bains' house owned. Tam crossed the lane twice and did not come in either time. And from the wharf there rose, now and then, the sudden strange hush of men stopping a talk all at once because the one thing they meant not to mention had entered it anyway.

Mairi was done waiting for the village to become useful.

Ewan had not spoken again. The effort seemed to have cost him dearly. He drifted in and out of a strained stillness that was not sleep and not waking either, his skin cool, the shell at his throat faintly damp-looking no matter how dry the room remained. The tide-sounds had quieted near dawn, but only in the way a creature quiets when listening better. The salt arc across the floor was still there in thin white interruption, and by daylight Mairi could no longer pretend it did not describe a shape.

A joining, Ailie had called it.

Mairi had not forgiven the phrase.

Reverend Sutherland had gone before midnight with the papers wrapped back in cloth, promising to search the remaining chest at first light for anything touching the old houses, the church ground, or the private Calder notes. It had sounded like a promise made by a man who had discovered too late that prudence and cowardice often wore the same coat. Ailie had gone too, but only after making Mairi swear that no one would move Ewan's bed, lift the floorboards, or lay him elsewhere in the house.

"Swear it," she had said.

"I am not a child."

"Nor am I asking one."

So Mairi had sworn.

Now she stood at the kitchen table tying her shawl with fingers too stiff from bad rest and worse temper, while Mrs. Kincaid watched from the stove with that expression women reserved for other women behaving unreasonably in ways they could not quite call wrong.

"You're not leaving him."

"I am."

"No."

Mairi looked up. "That was not a request for judgment."

"You'll have it anyway. You look half dead yourself."

"Then perhaps I'll blend better with the harbor."

Mrs. Kincaid clicked her tongue sharply. "Don't make black jokes in a house already listening."

That stopped Mairi a moment.

The older woman, seeing the hit land, softened only enough to make the next words worse. "Where are you going?"

"To the wharf."

"For what?"

"For the truth Tam Bain could not bring to my table in August."

Mrs. Kincaid's face tightened. "You think men tell better lies in daylight?"

"I think they tell them worse when they have no time to prepare."

From the back room came the faint scrape of bedsheets. Mairi turned at once.

Ewan was awake, watching the doorway. There were shadows under his eyes now that no child ought to wear, and something in his face had changed with the speaking—not older, not exactly, but more effortful, as if language itself had become a shore too steep to climb casually. When Mairi went to the bed, he lifted one hand from the blanket and caught the edge of her sleeve.

"I'll not be long," she said.

His fingers tightened once.

"Mrs. Kincaid is here."

His gaze moved toward the wall.

"I know." Mairi bent and kissed his forehead. Cool. Less terrible than before. Still wrong. "I know."

He looked back at her then, and with his free hand he traced once in the air—not on paper this time, not with charcoal—the downward line he had made at the window two days before.

Below.

Mairi swallowed.

"Aye," she said quietly. "And I mean to learn what was above it first."

His grip loosened.

Mrs. Kincaid, at the kitchen door, pretended not to have seen. "I'll sit," she said gruffly. "And if the wall starts up again, I'll hear it."

"You needn't touch the bed," said Mairi.

"Who said I wanted to?"

That settled what could be settled.

Mairi went out into a morning made mean by low cloud and wind. The harbor looked rubbed raw. The Mouth was a strip of hard-moving grey between black stone lips, and the tide within the inner reach carried the faint oily shimmer of disturbed weather. Men were already at work, though with the restlessness that came of not trusting the day enough to commit themselves fully to it. Nets hung from racks in dark dripping lengths. A crate of cod was being sorted beside the main wharf. Two boys struggled with a coil of line too proud to behave. Somewhere a hammer struck wood three times, paused, and began again.

Conversations thinned as Mairi approached.

Not stopped entirely. That would have been too obvious. Greyhook was better mannered than that in its cruelties. But the sound altered. Men who had been speaking in full voice shifted to mutters. Backs turned a degree more than necessary. One fellow suddenly found the sole of his boot worthy of inspection. Another spat over the wharf rail and kept his eyes fixed on the water as if there were commandments in it.

Tam Bain stood by the net racks with Reid and Kincaid, his hands occupied with a tear he was mending badly because his eyes were not on the work. He saw Mairi at once. So did the others.

Reid said, "Morning, Mairi."

She did not return it. "Tam."

His jaw set.

"Come off," Kincaid muttered under his breath, not quite to either of them.

Tam laid down the net and wiped his hands slowly on his trousers, though there was nothing on them that needed wiping. "You should not be down here."

"And you should have told me the truth in August. We are both poorly placed."

Reid looked at Kincaid. Kincaid looked at the harbor. Neither moved away fast enough.

Tam said, "Not here."

"Where else? In my kitchen again, with all your decent phrases stacked round you like barrels? No."

A couple of men farther down the wharf had gone very still. One of the boys with the coil of line had frozen outright and was pretending not to listen so intently that he might as well have announced it.

Tam took one step toward her. "Mairi."

"No." She gave him the word back hard. "You are going to tell me, before whoever is nearest and gossip-hungriest, what happened the day Ewan went over."

His face blanched under beard and weather.

"Mairi," Reid said low, "this is no place."

She rounded on him. "And August was? September? The whole winter? Which place did you keep ready for truth, Mr. Reid?"

That shut him.

Tam's hands had curled at his sides. "You think I've not told myself that day enough for six men and a minister?"

"I think you've told yourself the version you could stand."

Something moved in his face then—not anger first, as she expected, but hurt. Real hurt, old and exhausted.

Good, she thought savagely. Let it.

"Come," he said at last.

He did not mean away from the harbor entirely. Only as far as the lower edge of the net sheds where the sound of the water against the pilings and the leather flap of hanging gear could swallow some words and distort others. It was not privacy. Greyhook had little of that. But it was at least a place where men could pretend not to hear if they were feeling charitable.

Mairi followed. Reid and Kincaid did not, though neither went far.

Tam stood half-turned from the water, as if not willing to give his back wholly to land or sea. The habit of men who had spent years dividing themselves.

"Well?" said Mairi.

For a moment he said nothing. Wind moved through the netting above them with a sound like rough cloth drawn across old splinters.

Then: "It was not rough when we went out."

She kept still.

"Cloudy, aye. A lift in the swell farther off. But not rough. Not wrong enough to keep in."

"Yet you told me the water turned ugly."

"It did."

"When?"

He scrubbed one hand over his mouth. "Later."

"How much later?"

"After noon. Maybe before. You know how it is outside the Mouth when the light sits flat."

"I know how men lose time when truth wants measuring."

That struck. He ignored it with effort.

"We were on the west side of the grounds first. Poor enough catch there. Ewan was quiet all morning."

"He was not a babbling child."

"I didn't say he was."

No, she thought. But you thought it.

Tam went on. "He'd been watching the water."

"What water?"

He gave her a quick angry look. "The sea, Mairi. The one there is."

"That is not enough for you to mean."

His nostrils flared. "The patch beyond the outer line. Eastward. Not where we meant to drift, only where the current set us after the second line fouled."

There. At last. Something not in the August account.

"You did drift."

"A little."

"You said no such thing."

"Because it made no matter to the loss."

"Didn't it?"

Tam looked at the water and said nothing.

Mairi felt the old rage sharpening itself bone by bone. "What did Ewan say?"

At that he truly startled. "How did you know he said anything?"

Because my son came back with the sea in his throat, she thought. Because he has been drawing what you would not name. Because you have worn one withheld sentence across your face since summer.

"He said something," she repeated.

Tam closed his eyes once.

"When the line fouled," he said slowly, "he was at the stern quarter. Not in the way. Watching over. I thought he was looking at birds."

"There were birds?"

"No."

The answer hung there.

"He said, 'Uncle Tam.' Just like that. Quiet. I turned. He pointed."

"To what?"

Tam swallowed visibly. "At the water."

"That water again."

"Aye."

"And?"

"He asked, 'What's down there?'"

Mairi's hands went cold despite the wind.

"What did you tell him?"

"What was there to tell? I said nothing was down there but depth and rock if you were unlucky."

"And he believed you?"

"No."

That came quick and flat.

Tam drew breath through his nose and let it out harder. "He said it looked like posts."

The word struck cleanly through her.

Posts. Uprights. The strokes beneath the sign.

"What kind of posts?"

"How should I know?" Tam snapped, then caught himself and lowered his voice. "I saw only water."

"Did you?"

He stared at her. For a second she thought he would refuse again, would put the lie back on like an old coat and turn from her into the safety of weather and rope and the common cruelty of accidents.

Instead he said, "Not at first."

Mairi did not move.

"Not at first," he repeated, quieter now, as if once admitted the truth wanted gentler handling. "I looked where he pointed and saw only the sheen on it. Flat light. Current wrong a little. Then the boat shifted and the water changed its face."

She hated the phrase. Loved it, too, because it was a phrase a truthful man would arrive at reluctantly.

"How?"

Tam's eyes had gone far away.

"Like there was shape beneath it. Pale. Not surf. Not foam. I thought for a blink it was wreckage. Uprights. Something man-made where no man-made thing should stand."

"A mast?"

"No. More than one. Too close-set. And then gone."

He rubbed hard at his beard as if trying to scour the memory loose. "I looked at Ewan then. He looked pleased."

Mairi stared.

"Pleased?"

"Not happy. Not grinning. Only—" Tam broke off, disgusted with language. "As if he'd seen something that made sense of a question he'd had and was glad of it."

My son, she thought with sudden desperate pain, because that was him exactly. The look he had worn over odd knots, trapped fish, bent hinges—anything that revealed an inner use when others saw only object.

"Then what happened?"

"The line jerked. Hard. Not on a fish. Like it had caught under. We all turned to it. Reid shouted. I moved for the hook. The boat gave one swing—one only—and Ewan stepped where there was no deck."

Mairi's mouth opened, but no words came for a moment.

"Stepped where there was no deck?"

Tam nodded once, miserable and furious both. "His foot went over clean. Not slipped. Not pitched. Stepped."

"As if—"

"As if he thought there was more boat there." Tam looked at her then with such naked strain that for one instant the years between them collapsed into simple human damage. "Do you think I've not said that to myself?"

"Why didn't you tell me?"

"Because what mother would hear it and keep her wits? Because what man would say, I watched your son step after something I did not understand into a place where the water looked built wrong?"

The answer was not cowardly enough to satisfy her. That made it worse.

"You went after him."

"Aye."

"How fast?"

"Fast as I could."

"Fast enough?"

He flinched as if struck.

"I had him once."

The words were almost inaudible.

Mairi felt her whole body go still around them.

"What?"

Tam's voice roughened. "His jacket. Not him. I had cloth in my hand and then I had only cloth."

Mairi shut her eyes.

"I shouted. Reid saw the splash by then. Kincaid was hauling line. I went over to my waist. Another foot and I'd have gone too." His gaze dropped to his own hand, as though the old rope-burn might yet be visible there. "The water was colder than it had any right to be. Like a pocket of cellar-dark under summer sea."

"And then?"

"And then nothing. No second sight of him. No cry. No hand. We circled. We dragged. We searched till weather turned enough that Reid said if we stayed we'd make two losses and one widow more." He looked up sharply. "You think I left him easy?"

Mairi did not answer that.

Because the truth was worse. She could see now that he had not left Ewan easily. He had left him necessarily, which was less forgivable in the heart and more forgivable in the world, and therefore crueler than either.

"What did the others see?"

"Enough."

"Enough what?"

Tam's jaw tightened. "Reid saw the water move wrong. Kincaid heard a bell."

"A bell."

"So he says."

"There was no bell."

"No."

"Then why did none of you say this?"

Tam laughed then, a short cracked thing with no mirth in it. "And to whom would we say it? To the minister? To your face? To our own wives and have the whole village looking east of the grounds with old stories woke in them?" He stepped nearer, not threateningly but because the words wanted less distance. "Mairi, men can live with weather. We can live with rope parting, boards giving, a foot missed in spray. What we cannot live with is the sea beginning to mean."

That silenced even her.

Beyond the shed, someone shouted for a gaff. A gull cried overhead with that harsh human-sounding contempt gulls had. The whole harbor continued, but at some slant from where they stood, as if truth had stepped them aside from the day.

Mairi said, more quietly, "And after?"

Tam knew what she meant.

"After we turned in, we agreed."

"On what?"

"On the order of it. The line fouled. The boat swung. The footing went bad. The water had gone rough. He was over before we could take him back." He met her eyes and did not look away this time. "Every piece of it true enough to stand. None of it whole."

Mairi thought of Reverend Sutherland and his careful phrases. Of Ailie's old women and older walls. Of the kirk chest with its cut pages and margin-signs. Of Ewan drawing uprights below the sea and graves below the kirk and the room itself turning into a map around his bed.

"You agreed," she said.

"Aye."

"With whose idea?"

Tam's mouth twisted. "Mine first. Then everybody's."

There it was. Not villainy. Not sacrifice. The simpler, commoner sin: men frightened enough to choose the version they could carry home.

Mairi looked at him a long moment.

"Do you know what he said last night?"

Tam went still. "He spoke?"

"One word."

"What?"

"Below."

The color went from Tam's face as cleanly as if the wind had stripped it.

He looked toward the church on the rise though he could not see it from there. Then toward the east, beyond the harbor mouth, beyond the line of working water, toward whatever patch of sea he had taught himself not to remember directly.

"Mairi," he said, and she heard now that what stood in his voice was not just fear but pleading. "Do not tell that in the village."

"Why?"

"Because they'll begin joining things."

She almost smiled then, though it came hard and joyless. "Too late."

Tam stared at her. "What does that mean?"

She looked past him, toward the wharf pilings, toward the under-harbor dark where water moved in short hard surges.

"It means the house has started listening back."

He did not ask what that meant. Or perhaps he knew better than to ask in public where words once said could not be called in whole again.

Instead he said, "What do you want of me now?"

It was a fair question. Mairi disliked fair questions. They threatened to make a person answer honestly.

"The names," she said.

"Names?"

"Every man on the boat that day. Every man who saw wrong water and came home choosing weather instead."

Tam's expression closed a little. "Why?"

"Because I am done speaking to the version agreed among you."

He gave the names slowly, as if each carried weight: Reid. Kincaid. Jory MacAskill, who had been on the aft line till noon. And wee Davie Crowe for half the day, though the boy had been put ashore before the drift.

Mairi fixed them all in mind.

Then: "And one more thing."

Tam's mouth hardened. "There's always one more thing."

"When he pointed—before he went over—where exactly were you?"

Tam hesitated. "East of the old grounds."

"Not enough."

He pressed thumb and forefinger to his brow. "You know the water where the outer sounding should drop clean?"

She nodded once.

"We were south of that. Near the line old men used to avoid in fog."

"What line?"

He looked at her and immediately regretted answering.

"The Holding line," he said.

The word seemed to arrive in the air already old.

Mairi kept herself from reacting only by force.

Holding.

Not shoal. Not reef. Not depth. Holding.

The mark on the paper. The minister's margin. The room's joining arcs. The old notes about certain houses taking the tide.

"What is the Holding line?"

Tam stared at her, almost angry now. "Do not start asking me old names as if I'm some shore-crone with stories in my apron."

"You just gave me one."

He made a rough dismissive motion. "It's what old men call a patch of wrong current where you don't linger. That's all."

"That is not all."

"No," he said, tired all at once. "Likely not."

They stood in silence then, the kind that follows not the end of talk but its admission that the next step is worse.

At last Mairi said, "If the minister or the doctor asks, you will tell them what you told me."

Tam laughed once in disbelief. "You think men speak the same truth twice?"

"I think they can be made to."

He rubbed one hand over the back of his neck. "And if I don't?"

Mairi looked at him steadily.

"Then I tell Greyhook what you agreed to say and what you did not."

The threat landed exactly as she meant it to.

Tam closed his eyes for one second and opened them again. "You'd scorch every man on that boat."

"I'd scorch every lie between my son and what took him."

For a moment he looked almost proud of her. That made her hate him freshly.

Then a voice called from the far side of the wharf, "Tam! You coming or not?"

He glanced over his shoulder.

When he looked back, something had settled in him. Not peace. Not surrender. A kind of grim acceptance men found when weather made the next task plain whether welcome or not.

"I'll tell it," he said. "Once."

"You'll tell it straight."

"As straight as I've got."

Mairi nodded.

She turned to go and had taken only three steps when Tam said behind her, "Mairi."

She stopped but did not look back.

"I never thought him dead," he said.

That undid something in her more effectively than tears might have. She stood with the wharf wind on her face and the whole listening village at her back and could not answer because if she did she might say something that would remain forever between them.

So she walked on.

Up from the sheds. Past the fish tables. Past men suddenly intent on knots and crates and boots. Past Mrs. Kincaid's cousin pretending to mend a basket in full weather for no reason but eavesdropping. Up toward the lane and the kirk rise beyond it.

At the corner by the cooper's shed, Reverend Sutherland was coming down from the church with a wrapped parcel under one arm and Dr. Calder at his side.

They had the look of men who had been speaking soberly and had found no comfort in it.

When they saw Mairi's face, both stopped.

The minister said, "You've spoken with Tam."

"Yes."

Calder's eyes narrowed. "And?"

Mairi drew one breath.

"He saw posts under the water. Ewan did first. There was a bell where no bell was. And the men agreed a better story before they reached the harbor."

Neither man spoke at once.

Then Sutherland said softly, "Aye."

Not surprise. Recognition.

Calder looked between them, impatient already. "Aye? You say that as if the words were waiting for you."

Sutherland tightened his hold on the wrapped parcel. "Not waiting. Threatened."

Mairi's eyes went to the bundle. "What is that?"

"From the lower vestry chest," said the Reverend. "A plan."

"What sort of plan?"

He hesitated.

Dr. Calder, who had less practice than ministers in disguising alarm with caution, answered for him.

"Of the old church ground," he said. "And what stood there before."

7

The Old Ground

The wind had shifted by the time they reached Mairi's house, and with it the village mood.

News moved differently when carried downhill from the kirk than up from the wharf. Wharves bred rumor by salt and appetite; kirk yards gave it shape. Men who would shrug off a fisher's tale as weather-talk went quieter when the minister himself was seen coming down from the rise with his coat unbuttoned, a wrapped bundle under one arm, and Dr. Hugh Calder keeping pace beside him like a man who had ceased pretending to dislike his own curiosity.

By the time they entered Mairi's kitchen, Greyhook had begun not merely to listen but to arrange itself for listening.

Mairi shut the door hard behind them.

"Show me."

Reverend Sutherland set the parcel on the table with more care than its wrapping seemed to merit. It was oil-cloth gone stiff at the folds, tied with thin cord, and damp at one corner from weather or old storage. Calder stripped off his gloves and stood near the lamp, restless in every joint. He had the look of a man who had spent the walk from the kirk asking questions and being given fewer answers than his pride considered fair.

Mrs. Kincaid came from the back room before Mairi could call for her, wiping her hands on her apron.

"Well?"

"No," said Mairi.

"No what?"

"No asking all at once."

Mrs. Kincaid drew herself up. "I'll ask in my own order, thank you."

But she held.

From the back room came no sound.

That, more than any noise, made Mairi uneasy. The tide in the walls had gone quiet since she left for the harbor. Ewan had been left with Mrs. Kincaid, the room barred against well-meaning hands and village nerves alike, and if she had expected anything on her return it had been some new escalation—more salt, more sound, another word dragged through his ruined throat. Instead the house had taken on the terrible composure of something waiting to see what the living would bring into it next.

Sutherland untied the cord.

Inside lay a folded sheet, heavier than paper and thinner than proper board, made from some old drafting stock gone soft with age. Along with it were three smaller scraps and a narrow page torn from a different book, its edges browned and ragged as peat. The minister laid them all out beneath the lamp.

Mairi reached for the large folded sheet.

"Careful," Calder said at once.

She shot him a look sharp enough to have taken skin if looks were tools. "Do not begin."

He had the grace to lift both hands and retreat a half-inch.

The sheet opened in cracking stages.

It was a plan indeed—not of the church as it stood, but of the rise itself. The drawing had been made in a competent narrow hand, lines ruled where needed, notes entered along the edges in faded iron-brown ink. It showed the present kirk, small and square on its rise. The marked burial ground about it. The path from the lane. The old stone boundary in broken line. But beneath and beyond these, in lighter ink and a different hand, were older outlines.

Rectangles. Post-lines. A curve or hooked shape below the rise toward the village side. And farther down, closer to where Greyhook's first houses might once have stood, a cluster of marks not labeled at all.

"What am I looking at?" said Mairi.

"The formal plan was made when the burial ground was widened," said Sutherland. "About forty years ago."

"And the rest?"

"Added later. Or earlier and copied over, it is difficult to say."

Calder leaned in, one finger hovering over the lighter marks without touching them. "This is not church work."

"No," said Sutherland.

"What, then?"

The minister's mouth thinned. "Something noted and not embraced."

Ailie Crowe, who had not been in the room a moment earlier and was now somehow present in the doorway with her shawl damp at the hem, said, "That's kirk talk for theft with a prayer before it."

No one asked when she had come in. The house had ceased to be the sort of place where entrances required accounting.

Mairi looked from the sheet to the old woman. "You knew."

"I suspected."

"That is a village disease."

"Aye," said Ailie. "And still better than your minister's line in concealment."

Sutherland accepted the blow with the bleak patience of a man who had already spent the walk down from the kirk administering worse to himself.

He pointed to the lighter outlines. "These were identified in one of the side notes as the old ground."

"The old ground," said Mrs. Kincaid. "That tells us a great deal."

"It tells us what it was called," said Calder.

"By whom?"

Sutherland slid one of the smaller scraps forward. "By this hand."

The scrap was nearly illegible at first glance, the ink furred and broken. But the key words stood enough to be read.

...the old ground below the Christian burials......posts or standing works under the soil......not to be opened again absent necessity...

Mairi looked up sharply. "Opened."

"Yes," said Sutherland.

"Opened for what?"

"No reason is given."

Ailie laughed once, without humor. "Then there was a reason worth hiding."

Calder bent closer to the larger sheet. "These marks here," he said, tracing the lighter cluster with the edge of his nail, "they run under the later burial rows."

"Under?" said Mairi.

He looked up. "If the scale is right."

Sutherland answered before she could. "It is right enough."

The room held still.

Church ground. The graves Ewan had drawn. The chest beside them. And now something older lying below the Christian burials like a memory no one had finished covering properly.

Mairi said, "The room."

No one spoke.

"The room in my house," she said more sharply. "Ewan drew the room. He drew the sign where the arcs met. Then the graves. Then the chest. If this old ground lies under the burial rows, why is my house hearing it?"

Ailie moved to the table then, her hands resting lightly on the wood as if she mistrusted the floor more.

"Because old places do not stay where men write them," she said. "They get broken, taken apart, carried into sheds and houses and kirk repairs. A beam goes here, a hinge there, a footing stone under a threshold, and after three generations no one knows where the first shape ended."

Mrs. Kincaid frowned at the plan. "Then this is not one place."

"No," said Ailie. "It was one place once. That is not the same thing."

Calder, who had been trying very hard not to side openly with Ailie Crowe on anything, said reluctantly, "Distributed structure."

Mrs. Kincaid turned to stare at him. "That's your grand version of broken old timber?"

"It is the correct version."

"It is a pompous version."

"It is accurate."

Ailie said, "And still less useful than mine."

Mairi let them snap past one another because her mind had caught on one phrase in the scrap and would not release it.

"Standing works," she said.

Sutherland nodded.

"The posts Tam saw."

"Perhaps."

"Not perhaps." The word came harder than she intended. "He said Ewan saw them first. Under the water. Uprights where no uprights should be."

Calder's eyes moved at once to the plan again. "If there were structures here once—older than the church, older than the village proper—and if some part of them lay lower on the rise or nearer the harbor edge..."

"Then what?" said Mairi.

He exhaled. "Then the same geometry may exist in more than one register. Land. Water. The room."

Mrs. Kincaid looked scandalized. "Geometry."

"That is the least offensive word available."

"The least useful too."

Ailie, unexpectedly, gave Calder the slightest nod. "No. He's near enough there."

Mairi was done with near enough.

"What were they?" she said. "These standing works. These posts. This old ground. Pick whichever name offends you least and tell me what it was."

No one answered.

Because no one knew.

That enraged her more than if they had lied.

She put both hands on the table and leaned over the plan until her shadow fell across it. "Then I will tell you what I have. My son went over near a place the men called the Holding line. He returned with shell under his skin and maps in his hand. The walls in his room hear water though the plaster's dry. Salt is tracing shapes across the floor. He drew graves before any of you had the courage to say church ground aloud. And when he spoke, he said below." She looked from face to face. "So tell me whether I have brought him home to the wrong house, or whether Greyhook itself was built on the wrong grave."

The force of it drove even Mrs. Kincaid quiet.

At length Reverend Sutherland said, very carefully, "Both may be true."

The kitchen seemed to shrink around that.

From the back room came a sharp knock.

Not at the door. Not from the wall.

From within the room itself.

All four adults turned.

Then came a second knock, lower and woodier, as if something beneath the bed had struck once against board.

Mrs. Kincaid went white. “No.”

Mairi was already moving.

She reached the doorway first and stopped hard enough that Sutherland behind her nearly struck her shoulder.

The room looked ordinary.

That was the worst of it.

The lamp still burned low on the shelf. The bed remained where it had been. Ewan lay on his side facing the wall, blanket drawn to his throat. Nothing had overturned. Nothing had burst or seeped or broken.

Then Mairi saw the floor.

The salt lines had advanced.

No longer thin and accidental at the seams, they now described most of the broad arc Ewan had drawn—one line from the bed-wall, one from the opposite side, curving inward toward the room’s center. Where they neared one another, near the foot of the bed, the wood had darkened in a patch the size of a washbasin as if wetness stood just beneath it and had not yet decided to come through.

“Do not step there,” said Ailie quietly behind them.

Mairi did not need telling. Every instinct she had recoiled from the darkened patch.

Ewan turned his head.

His eyes were open and too clear.

“Ewan,” Mairi said.

He lifted one hand from the blanket and pointed not to the floor, not to the wall, but to the blanket box at the bed's foot.

For a moment she did not understand.

Then came the third knock.

Inside the box.

Mrs. Kincaid gave a little cry and clapped a hand over her mouth.

Calder said, "Dear God."

Sutherland did not speak.

Mairi crossed herself before she could stop herself, then hated the reflex on sight.

The blanket box was plain pine, scarred from years of use, its lid warped a little on one side where damp had gotten into the grain two winters ago. It held old clothes, summer blankets, a pair of Ewan's too-short boots Mairi had not yet given away, and three things belonging to her dead husband that she had not wanted out in daily sight.

Nothing inside should knock.

"Open it," said Calder.

Ailie said at once, "No."

Mairi stood between the two commands as if they had been hands pulling opposite sleeves.

"Why not?" Calder demanded.

"Because if it's using the room, you do not start answering every knock like a fool."

"And if something inside is shifting because the floor is settling under it—"

Ailie turned on him. "And if your hand on the lid is all it needs?"

They glared at each other.

Mrs. Kincaid whispered, "You'll split me in two with this."

Mairi ignored them both and looked to Ewan.

"Do you want it opened?"

His eyes moved to hers, then to the box, then back. His face tightened in visible effort. Once more his mouth worked.

This time the word came like rust on a hinge.

"No."

Mairi shut her eyes briefly.

There, then.

She turned to Calder. "No."

He made a sound of sharp frustration but did not argue further.

Sutherland said, "Get it out of the room."

Ailie's head snapped toward him. "Without opening?"

"If possible."

"Possible," said Ailie, "is doing heavy work tonight."

But Mairi saw at once that he was right. Whatever the box contained mattered less than where it sat: at the foot of the bed, near the darkening patch, inside the shape being traced across the room.

"Tam," she said aloud, though he was not there.

Mrs. Kincaid flinched. "I'll send for him."

"No. Stay."

Mairi handed her the lamp instead. "If I say move, you move. If I say leave, you leave. And if he"—she nodded toward Calder—"tries to open it, bite him."

Mrs. Kincaid, to her credit, nodded as if this were all perfectly reasonable household management.

Calder said, "I am still here."

"Yes," said Mairi. "That is the difficulty."

Together she and Sutherland took the box, one at either end. The wood was heavier than it should have been. Not impossibly so. Only by that small wrong margin which told the body before the mind that an object had acquired some extra claim on the world.

The moment they lifted it, the dark patch on the floor gave a soft sound like water released from a cupped hand.

Mairi nearly dropped her end.

"Steady," said Sutherland through his teeth.

They carried the box backward, careful not to cross the salt arcs more than they had to, and set it down in the kitchen just beyond the threshold.

At once the tide-sound resumed in the room.

Not violent. Not angry.

Stronger.

As if whatever had paused to consider the box's presence had now decided it was not, after all, the point.

Ewan shut his eyes and made the rough throat-catch again.

Mairi went to him at once. "Does it hurt?"

He blinked once.

Yes.

That undid her patience.

She turned, furious suddenly at all of them—at Calder with his useful uselessness, at Sutherland with his careful inherited omissions, at Ailie with her maddening fragments, at Greyhook for being built of old theft and older silence, and perhaps most of all at herself for standing in the room while her son was made into some measure for the village's buried shape.

"What now?" she said.

No one answered immediately.

Then Ailie, still at the threshold and not crossing it, looked not at the floor nor at the walls but at the plan on the kitchen table.

"We follow the chest."

Sutherland stared at her. "What?"

"The one he drew," she said, jerking her chin toward Ewan. "Beside the graves."

Calder said, "You think there is an actual chest under the churchyard?"

Ailie's face remained dry and hard. "I think there was one, or is one, or something men called one because they'd no better word. Kept. Moved. Buried. Bound into the ground under proper burial after."

"That is absurd."

"No," said Sutherland, and for the first time there was something almost fierce in his voice. "It is exactly the sort of thing men before me would have done."

The room went still around him.

He seemed not to notice that he had spoken aloud one of the sharper truths in his keeping.

Mairi said, "Then we go to the church."

Mrs. Kincaid made a sound halfway between protest and prayer.

Calder said, "In this weather? At night?"

"Was the sea polite enough to begin in daylight?"

"That is not the point."

"It is to me."

Sutherland looked toward the window. Outside, dusk had thickened into a black-blue evening with rain beginning in slant lines too fine to hear yet. "The ground will be poor."

Ailie said, "The ground has been poor for longer than the weather."

Mairi ignored them all and bent to Ewan.

"If I go to the church, do I go right?"

He opened his eyes. For one second she feared he would not answer at all.

Then he lifted two fingers, slowly, and pointed—not toward the kirk itself, but lower, as if beneath it.

Below.

Again.

Mairi drew back and stood.

"That is enough."

Calder stared at her. "Enough for what?"

"To stop asking whether."

Sutherland gathered the old plan and the loose scraps, not hurriedly but with the grave economy of a man who had crossed from uncertainty into obligation and knew it. "I will get shovels."

Mrs. Kincaid said, "You will do no such thing without men."

"Yes," said the Reverend. "I know."

"And not half the village either," Ailie added. "Unless you fancy twenty stories by dawn and none of them useful."

Calder gave a short bitter laugh. "Useful seems not to be an available category in Greyhook."

"Then make yourself one," said Ailie.

He looked at her, and something in his face almost yielded to admiration before pride covered it over again.

Mairi tightened her shawl and looked once more at her son.

The shell at his throat gleamed faintly in the lamplight. His face had gone drawn with effort. But his eyes were fixed on her, and in them now there was no wandering depth at all. Only urgency. Only trust.

That nearly broke her.

Instead it hardened her into motion.

"We go quietly," she said. "No bell. No neighbors. Tam, if he can be had. No one else unless needed."

Mrs. Kincaid set the lamp down with a firm hand. "Then I'm needed."

"No."

"Yes."

Mairi opened her mouth to refuse again, but Mrs. Kincaid's expression had moved beyond argument into that stony maternal territory where permission no longer mattered.

Ailie said, "I'm coming."

"That I expected," said Mairi.

Sutherland wrapped the papers again and tucked them under his arm. Calder closed his black case with a snap as if the gesture might restore the world to categories. No one believed it would.

And in the back room, behind the dry plaster and beneath the darkened boards, the tide came in once more—patient, measured, as if it knew very well they had only just begun to answer it.

8

The Church Below

They did not go by the main path.

That was Reverend Sutherland's idea, and Mairi respected it chiefly because it was the first practical thing he had offered that did not arrive wrapped in apology. The front lane up to the kirk was too open, too visible from house windows, too likely to catch the eye of any sleepless soul in Greyhook inclined to see a lantern moving where no lantern ought to be moving and improve a story before dawn had the chance. So they went by the back way: a narrower track running behind the Kincaids' shed, past the old cooper's lean-to, up through the scrubby rise where salt grass gave way to stone and hard earth.

Tam joined them at the lane corner without a word.

Mairi had sent Mrs. Kincaid's eldest for him, and he had come quickly enough that she knew he had been expecting the summons whether or not he admitted it. He carried two shovels over one shoulder and a mattock in the other hand. Rain had darkened his coat at the seams. When his eyes met Mairi's there was no request in them to be forgiven, only a grim willingness to keep walking in the direction she pointed.

Good, she thought. Forgiveness was a soft-weather thing.

The company was small, just as she had ordered: Mairi, Tam, Reverend Sutherland, Dr. Calder, Old Ailie Crowe, and Mrs. Kincaid, who had brought a lantern and the kind of resolve no one was likely to move with words alone.

No one spoke much on the climb.

The wind pressed at them from the harbor side, carrying the smell of wet rope, kelp, and distant fish offal from the wharf. Behind those ordinary village scents lay another note that Mairi had come to know too well over the last two days: that cold mineral tang like salt laid on old stone below tide line. She would have sworn it was stronger here, though whether from the weather or from the rise toward the kirk she could not tell.

The church appeared in pieces through the dark.

First the low boundary stones. Then the pale shoulder of the kirk wall. Then the small black cut of the windows. Then the leaning rows of slate markers in the burying ground, each one catching lantern-light for a breath and releasing it again.

The place had never frightened Mairi before.

Not because she lacked reverence, but because Greyhook's dead had always seemed, if not companionable, then settled. The kirk yard was part of the village's order. You buried what the sea returned and what fever kept. You set the stone if money allowed and the ground held. You visited on the right Sundays. You did not ask more of the dead than stillness, and they generally obliged.

Tonight the churchyard did not feel settled.

It felt layered.

That was the difference. Not haunting, not menace from the headstones themselves, but the sense of one order laid over another with too little separation between them.

Sutherland unlocked the side door and ushered them into the vestry room first, not the kirk proper. The little chamber smelled of damp wool, lamp oil, paper, and old wood that had weathered so many winters it had lost any interest in pretension. A table stood against one wall. Shelves above it held registers, hymnals gone soft with use, and two cracked collection boxes. In the corner sat the side chest from which he had taken the plan earlier, its lid still open as if the room itself had been interrupted mid-thought.

He set down the wrapped papers and looked at each of them in turn.

"We dig once," he said. "Not half the yard. Not until we know whether the mark means anything more than fear making patterns of old notes."

Ailie gave him a long dry look. "You've brought shovels to a graveyard in the rain past midnight with five witnesses and a doctor. The time to speak as if you're uncertain has gone by."

Calder, taking off his wet gloves finger by finger, said, "It would still be pleasant if one of you decided on a theory before I am expected to stand in the mud over it."

Mrs. Kincaid answered, "Aye, and it would be pleasant if tea poured itself. We are not in pleasant times."

Tam leaned the shovels by the wall. His eyes had gone to the open chest in the corner and stayed there.

"What is that?"

"The side chest," said Sutherland. "For weather notes, parish scraps, memorial papers."

"That is not what I mean."

Everyone looked.

Tam was not staring at the chest as such, but at the floor beneath it.

Mairi moved closer with the lantern.

The boards there were old, narrower than the newer flooring near the table. One plank along the wall showed a slight dark bowing at the grain, and in the seam beside it lay a pale trace no church vestry ought to contain.

Salt.

"Do not tell me," Mrs. Kincaid whispered.

No one had the energy to oblige.

Calder crouched at once, touched the seam, and rubbed the grains between finger and thumb with a physician's fury at the world for not staying in proper categories.

"It is salt."

Ailie said, "We had this marvel earlier."

Sutherland had gone pale enough that the silver at his temples looked brighter. "This room was repaired sixteen years ago after the north leak."

Ailie turned toward him sharply. "With what timber?"

He blinked, then looked genuinely angry—at himself, perhaps, for hearing the sense of the question. "From the old storage shed."

"Which stood where?"

He did not answer.

Tam did.

"Lower side of the yard," he said. "Near the drop."

Mairi felt the plan rearranging itself in her head: the church on the rise, the later burials, the lower cluster of old marks beneath. The room in her house. The old storage shed. Reused timber.

Joining.

The word had become hateful now because it fit too well.

Sutherland took up the plan again and spread it on the vestry table under the lamp. This time he traced the lower cluster without hesitation.

"The old notes identify this part of the rise as prior ground." His finger moved to a narrow rectangle near the cluster. "And this structure here, whatever it once was, stood partly where the shed later stood."

"A chest house," said Ailie.

Calder looked up. "A what?"

"Not a house to live in," she said impatiently. "A place to keep."

"To keep what?"

She shrugged once. "If I knew that, we'd all be warmer."

Mairi leaned over the plan. "Where do we dig?"

No one answered immediately.

Then Tam pointed with the blunt end of the mattock, not at the church proper and not among the newer stones, but lower down the rise toward the back boundary where the ground sloped away toward the lane and the harbor beyond. There, half-hidden now by coarse grass and two crooked weather-worn markers, was a patch of ground with no stone over it at all.

"Here," he said.

"Why?"

"Because I remember the old shed footing." He frowned, dragging memory up from some place where boys' labor and weather had buried it. "There was always one corner stone that sat wrong. Grandfather said never lever it out, because the ground there 'held badly.'"

Held.

Mairi did not miss the word.

Sutherland folded the plan sharply. “Then we go there.”

The burying ground accepted them badly.

Rain had begun in earnest by then—not pounding, but steady enough to silver the slate stones and sink into wool collars and cuffs. Their lanterns moved in yellow pockets through the dark. Wet grass brushed at hems. The earth underfoot was slick where moss and old footpaths met. The whole yard smelled of rain, cold stone, turned soil, and something older under all three.

Mairi had been in churchyards by night before, after deaths, after storms, after the sea returned men too late for daylight nicety. But never like this. Never with the sense that the ground itself was waiting to see whether they had come to disturb it properly or merely to embarrass themselves.

They found the place easily once Tam set them to it.

The old shed footing was gone above ground except for one rectangular stone lying nearly flush in the turf beside two newer graves. No marker stood over the patch itself. No cross. No slate. Only rain-dark grass and the slight unevenness of earth that had settled more than once.

“This was left unmarked,” Mairi said.

Sutherland answered, “Not every part of church ground is burial.”

Ailie, crouching to touch the edge of the old stone, said, "No. But every church learns where to bury over what it wishes forgotten."

Calder, who had brought a spade despite all his protests, looked from one to the other. "You speak as if every kirk in the province is built over some heathen chest and a bad conscience."

Ailie glanced up at him. "No. Just the unlucky ones."

Tam set the shovel blade in first.

The sound it made as it bit into the wet earth was ordinary enough to make Mairi furious with relief. Soil. Roots. Stones. Nothing more. He lifted one cut and threw it aside. Sutherland took the second spade and worked beside him. They dug not like grave-robbers, not even like men in haste, but with the careful force of those who know the ground they cut may soon need naming.

Mairi held the lantern. Mrs. Kincaid held the other and muttered under her breath—not prayers exactly, but the sort of domestic litany women compose when no approved language seems fitted to the work.

"Wet enough for beans, poor enough for digging, and not a decent reason for any of us to be here..."

Calder crouched at the edge of the hole as it deepened a foot, then more, his physician's hands now blackening with churchyard mud. Rain ran off his nose; he ignored it.

Nothing.

Then the sound changed.

Tam struck something below the spade that was not stone.

Not hollow exactly. Not timber exactly. A dull resistant knock.

All six heard it.

Tam froze. So did the rest.

Again, more carefully this time, he cut away soil with the blade edge. A dark line emerged under the wet earth. Straight. Worked.

"Wood," said Calder.

"Maybe," said Ailie.

Sutherland knelt and brushed with bare fingers. Mud slid away in brown slicks. Beneath it lay a plank or lid gone black with age and water, grain still visible where the edge had not wholly rotted. Iron showed at one corner—strapwork or a hinge, too eaten to identify cleanly.

A box.

Or what had once been one.

Mrs. Kincaid made a small sound like someone trying not to say *Lord preserve us* for the fifth time in one hour and failing by increments.

Calder leaned closer, all weariness burned out of him now by the uglier cleaner energy of discovery. "There is a container here."

Ailie said, "Do not say it as if you found a bird's nest."

"It is what it is."

"That has not yet been established."

Tam looked up from the hole, rain on his beard and grief old as August in his eyes. "It was the chest."

No one corrected him.

Mairi's mind had already leapt backward to Ewan's drawing: the graves, the box-shape, the sign beneath. If he had shown them this, if the room had been joining toward this, then whatever lay under Christian ground and old repair timber and village silence had not merely persisted. It had been working.

Sutherland brushed more mud away. On the upper surface of the wood, faint beneath age and rot, a carved mark began to show.

A circle. A crescent. A crossing line.

The sign.

Mairi spoke before she knew she meant to. "Do not open it."

All of them turned to her.

Why had she said it? Because of Ewan's voice by the blanket box: *No.* Because the room in her house was already listening. Because whatever men before them had buried had been buried under church ground for a reason that no page had fully preserved.

Calder rose from his crouch, muddy and shining-eyed. "Mrs. Bain, if the object relates to the condition in your house—"

"If?"

"—then we must know what is inside."

Ailie said, "Or perhaps that is the one thing we must not know in the dark with rain over us and bad ground under."

"It is a box in earth, not a demon at table."

Tam said, very quietly, "You didn't see the water that day."

Calder's mouth closed.

Sutherland remained kneeling in the mud with one hand on the exposed timber, looking like a man asked to choose which branch of a tree held less lightning.

"Perhaps," he said slowly, "we lift it without opening."

Ailie barked a joyless laugh. "And to where? Into your vestry? Into Mairi's kitchen? You think moving a kept thing is a lesser asking than unlatching it?"

"Then what do you propose?"

"That we mark where it lies and think before we prove ourselves fools."

Calder straightened fully. "By morning half the village will know we have dug in the churchyard."

"Not if you keep your face shut."

"I mean the hole, Mrs. Crowe."

That silenced even Ailie for a breath.

He was right. The ground could be covered again, but not so cleanly as to fool anyone with church eyes and a morning habit of graveside visits.

Mairi felt the argument moving toward action whether she liked it or not. That was what villages and men did when frightened: if thinking threatened to grow too large, they turned at once to handling.

Then the church bell rang.

Once.

Not from inside. Not by rope or hand.

A single muffled strike from somewhere beneath or beside the yard, as if metal long buried had answered the disturbance with one patient note.

Mrs. Kincaid cried out outright this time.

Tam stumbled backward from the hole.

Calder went white under the mud.

Only Ailie did not move, and that stillness frightened Mairi worse than panic would have.

The bell-note died into rain.

Then, from beneath the exposed chest—or from the soil around it, or the old timbers under all of it, no one could later say—came a low sound Mairi knew at once and hated perfectly.

A tide drawing in.

Not in her house now. Not in the wall behind Ewan's bed. Here.

Below the church.

The sound was faint but unmistakable, as if black water moved through chambers under the rise and was pleased to find itself remembered.

Sutherland crossed himself before catching the reflex and hating it. "Cover it."

Calder stared at him. "What?"

"Cover it now."

"We cannot simply—"

"We can and we will."

Tam had already seized his shovel and was pushing earth back into the hole with rough desperate motions. Mairi almost thanked him for not needing the order twice. Sutherland followed, using his hands first and then the spade. Mrs. Kincaid, trembling, kicked loose sods in with the side of her boot. Calder stood one paralyzed second longer, then began helping with an expression of open fury, as if rage at absurdity were all that kept his body moving.

Ailie alone stayed at the edge, listening.

Mairi turned on her. "Help!"

Ailie looked at her and said, "It was quieter when left."

Mairi had no answer for that terrible, useless truth.

So she bent and worked too, shoving wet soil and turf back over the exposed wood while rain flattened her hair and ran cold between her shoulders. The sign vanished first under mud, then the iron corner, then the lid itself. At last only the disturbed shape of the earth remained, ugly and obvious but no longer open.

The tide-sound lessened.

Not stopped. Lessened.

As if whatever lay below had accepted, for now, the return of cover.

All of them stood breathing hard in the rain.

Calder wiped mud from his brow with the back of one hand and left a blacker streak there than before. "This is madness."

Ailie answered, "No. Madness was digging it."

Tam looked toward the harbor though there was nothing to see beyond the kirk wall and dark. "What if the house worsens now?"

Mairi's stomach dropped.

Ewan.

All at once every second spent in the churchyard felt stolen from him.

"We go back," she said.

Sutherland nodded instantly. "At once."

Calder looked at the re-covered patch, at the church, at the disturbed ground around it. "And this?"

"Waits till daylight," said the Reverend. "Or longer."

Ailie gave him a bleak look. "You think daylight civilizes what's under church soil?"

"No," he said. "But it gives men fewer excuses to lie about what they're doing."

That, Mairi thought, was perhaps the truest thing he had said all night.

They did not bother with the side path on the way down. They moved quickly, lanterns swinging, boots slipping in mud, the village below them a handful of dark roofs and faint lights gathered tight against the harbor. As they descended, Mairi thought she heard—very faint and very far—a knocking carried through the rain.

Not from the church. Not from the lane.

From the direction of her house.

Inside her, something cold and maternal and merciless set itself like iron.

By the time they reached the Bains' door, she was running.

The latch gave under her hand. She crossed the kitchen in three strides and flung open the back-room door.

The lamp within still burned.

Mrs. Kincaid's shawl lay on the chair where she had left it.

The blanket box stood in the kitchen where they had set it earlier.

And on the floor of Ewan's room, the salt arcs had completed themselves.

At their meeting point, just below the bed and within the hinge-shape the room had been drawing all along, the boards were wet at last.

Not flooded. Not broken through.

Only wet, dark, and shining, as though some black seam beneath the house had answered what they had disturbed under the church and begun, patiently, to open.

9

The Hinge in the Room

No one entered at once.

They stood in the doorway like fools at the threshold of their own answer, lantern light striking the wet sheen on the floorboards and jumping back dull and yellow from the salt-white arcs that had at last completed their shape. The room was no longer merely marked. It was arranged.

The two curving lines met just below the bed in a darkened place no larger than a washbowl. The boards there shone as though damp had risen through them from below and paused at the surface out of courtesy. The wood around the patch had gone almost black. Not rotten. Not warped. Simply altered by saturation that should not have been possible in a room where the wall-plaster stood dry and the underside of the floor, if one followed ordinary reason, opened only to crawlspace, stones, and earth.

No one spoke.

Then Mairi saw the bed.

Not the room. Not the floor. The bed.

Ewan was not lying where she had left him.

He was still in it, yes. Still beneath the blanket. Still turned somewhat toward the wall. But the whole bed-frame had shifted a hand's breadth from its original place, drawn not outward into the room, but inward toward the wet meeting point of the arcs. So slightly that another eye might have missed it. Mairi did not.

Her body moved before thought did.

"Do not step there," Ailie said sharply behind her.

Mairi stopped with one foot raised.

The old woman came in at last, lantern lifted, and crouched at the threshold of the salt shape without crossing it. Her lined face had gone severe in a way that took even weather out of it.

"It's taking measure," she said.

Calder, furious at fear because fear had made him stand still in front of a child's bed, snapped, "Would all of you stop saying things as if they explain themselves?"

Ailie did not look round. "It explains enough."

"No, it does not. Nothing in this house explains enough."

Sutherland said, more quietly than either, "Hush."

That alone made Calder obey.

Because the room had changed again.

Not visibly. Not by any movement of wall or timber. But by sound.

The tide-noise Mairi had learned in the plaster was no longer behind the bed, nor in the opposite wall, nor spread thinly through the room at large. It now came from the wet place where the arcs met. A low inward wash. A pause. Then the same soft drag, as though black water moved somewhere just beneath the skin of the floorboards and turned itself in a narrow chamber.

The room had a center now.

Mairi kept her eyes on Ewan.

He was awake.

His face had gone drawn with effort, the mouth pale, the skin under the eyes shadowed dark. But when he saw her, something in his expression eased—not relief exactly, because relief belonged to the safe and the solved—but recognition fierce enough to hurt.

"I'm here," she said.

His eyes flicked, not to the wet patch, but to the wall beside the bed.

Then to her.

Then back.

A warning, perhaps. Or a request.

"Can you move him?" Calder said.

Ailie turned her head slowly toward him. "Across that?"

Calder's jaw tightened. "Around it, then."

"There is no around it."

He looked again and saw what Mairi had already seen. The completed arcs and the placement of the bed had turned the room into something like a marked threshold. To reach Ewan cleanly from the doorway meant crossing one of the salt lines at least, and likely the wet center once the frame had been shifted farther than it first appeared.

Sutherland said, "The head side."

Mairi followed his gaze. The only possible route lay along the narrow wall-side space between bed and plaster, where the original seam of salt had begun. Tight. Awkward. But perhaps passable if she climbed onto the bed or leaned across it.

"I go," she said.

"No," said Calder at once.

She did not even waste a look on him.

Ailie said, "Take the quilt chest."

"The box is in the kitchen."

"The chair, then. Something dry under your foot."

Mrs. Kincaid, who had been white-faced and silent since the churchyard, sprang suddenly useful. She fetched the chair from the kitchen, then hesitated at the threshold with it.

"Where?"

"There," said Ailie, indicating the bare strip just inside the door where salt had not yet touched.

Mrs. Kincaid set it down.

Mairi climbed onto the chair and from there onto the side rail of the bed, one hand on the wall, the other gripping the bedpost so hard the wood bit her palm. The mattress shifted under her weight. The wet place on the floor below gave a soft sound like breath drawn through teeth.

"Steady," Sutherland said.

"Be silent," said Mairi.

She knelt on the bed and reached Ewan.

His skin was cool—cooler than when she had left for the church—but not dead-cold. The shell at his throat gleamed faintly damp in the lamplight, the ridges more sharply defined now as if the hidden wet had climbed into them by some other route. When she slipped one arm behind his shoulders he flinched, not from her touch but from the room itself.

"What hurts?" she whispered.

He tried to lift his hand.

It trembled badly. She caught it and felt the strength in his fingers fail halfway through the gesture. His fingertips brushed once against her wrist, then turned toward the wall again.

The wall.

Mairi looked.

The faded paper beside the bed had bubbled ever so slightly outward in one place no larger than a man's palm.

Not water damage in the ordinary way. Not damp spreading. More as if something behind the paper had pressed once and retreated, leaving the surface lifted from lath by a pressure too local and too deliberate to call settling.

"There," she said.

Calder crowded the doorway farther, eyes narrowing. "What is it?"

"A blister," said Mrs. Kincaid faintly.

"On dry paper?" Calder muttered.

Ailie had gone still again. "Do not cut it."

"No one has said cut," said Sutherland, but weakly.

"No one needs to. I know a doctor's face when it wants a knife."

Calder opened his mouth and shut it.

Mairi shifted Ewan upright as far as she dared.

"We are moving him."

Ailie said, "No."

That stopped everyone.

Even Mairi.

"Why?" she demanded.

"Because he's the point."

Mrs. Kincaid made a broken sound of protest. "He's a child."

"Aye," said Ailie. "And the room's using him to hold shape."

Calder snapped, "You do not know that."

"Nor do you know the opposite."

Sutherland said, "If she moves him and the shape goes with him—"

Mairi rounded on him from the bed with such fury that he took a full step back. "Then say what you mean. Say it properly if you mean to keep my son in a room that is opening under him."

The minister, to his credit, did not retreat into piety or caution. He looked at the wet center, the salt arcs, the blistered patch of wall, then at Ewan's face.

"What I mean," he said quietly, "is that we may have one fixed point in this house, and if we pull it loose without knowing what is fastened through it, we may break the wrong thing open."

The truth of that sickened her because it sounded like the truth.

Ewan made a sound then.

Not a word. Barely voice. But enough to turn her back to him.

His eyes were fixed past her shoulder on the kitchen table.

On the wrapped papers from the kirk.

Mairi understood at once and hated that she did.

"The notes," she said. "He wants the notes."

Calder stared. "That is absurd."

"Then you explain his stare better."

No one could.

Sutherland brought the packet at once, which was the most sensible thing he had done all night. He spread the loose scraps and the plan on the bed near Mairi's knee, careful not to let any page slip toward the wet side.

Ewan's gaze moved over them, not aimlessly but with exhausted intent. He looked first at the old plan. Then at the scrap mentioning the old ground below the Christian burials. Then at a third paper none of them had yet truly examined—a narrow torn page in a different, earlier hand than the others.

"It was with the weather scraps," said Sutherland, seeing where the boy looked. "I had not read that one yet."

"Then read it now," said Mairi.

He picked it up and held it to the lamp.

The hand was cramped and older than the rest, the spelling uneven, the ink faded to a brown near the color of dried blood. He had to tilt the page twice before the lines resolved.

"What does it say?" Mairi asked.

Sutherland read slowly, the words catching at first in the age of their phrasing.

"'...the lower store being shifted from the old footings to the kirk rise, there was complaint after among the women that the back room of Bain's house—'"

He stopped.

All of them looked at him.

"Read," said Mairi.

He obeyed.

"'—the back room of Bain's house took damp in clear weather and gave sea-sounds on the turn, though the men would have it all from bad joinery and womanish nerves. Mr. Calder senior advised the marked plank from the lower store be removed, but this was not done, the householder saying sound wood was sound wood and no minister fed children on caution.'"

Tam said under his breath, "God help us."

Mairi's whole body had gone cold.

"Bain's house," she said.

Sutherland's eyes lifted from the page to hers. "Yes."

"Our house?"

"An older Bain house, almost certainly."

She could not seem to pull air low enough into her lungs.

Ailie said quietly, "There then."

Not triumph. Confirmation.

Calder said, "Continue."

Sutherland read on.

"'The sign cut on the plank matched the margin-note of the old keeping place and was thought by the old women to make a crossing if set wrong in a sleeping wall. It was ordered that the timber be turned or taken out entire, but no man undertook it, the weather being hard and the matter judged fit for postponement.'"

Mrs. Kincaid whispered, "Postponement."

Tam laughed once, raw with disgust. "That's a village word if ever one was."

Mairi looked toward the wall.

The blistered patch now seemed less like a wound than a memory surfacing through paper. A plank. A marked plank from the lower store. Set wrong in a sleeping wall.

"Which wall?" she said.

Sutherland turned the page in his hands, searching for more, but there was only one final line.

"'Best that no child be laid with the head to the marked side until proper work be done, else the room may take to measuring through the little living body, which is quickest led of all thresholds.'"

No one moved.

Mairi's hand tightened convulsively around Ewan's shoulder.

Threshold.

The room may take to measuring through the little living body.

She felt, rather than saw, Calder recoil inwardly from that line—not because it offended his intellect, but because it named too closely what the last two days had been showing him by force.

"Threshold," he repeated. "That is metaphor. Superstitious domestic language. It does not—"

"Do not," said Mairi.

He stopped.

"Do not make this smaller than it is because you came too late to name it first."

The rebuke landed.

Sutherland folded the page slowly. "The marked plank."

Ailie nodded once. "In the wall."

"The wall behind the bed," said Mairi.

No one disputed it.

Tam looked from the blistered paper to the wet floor and back. "Then we take it out."

Ailie swung on him. "And tear the hinge wider?"

"What else?"

Calder answered this time, grim now rather than skeptical. "If the timber is completing a crossing between the old structure and the room, removing it may collapse the present shape or release it."

Mrs. Kincaid stared at him. "Those are the same thing in a more educated coat."

He almost smiled. "Aye."

Mairi said, "Then we turn it."

All eyes went to her.

"The note said turned or taken out entire."

Sutherland frowned. "That is carpentry spoken in panic."

"It is still instruction."

Ailie considered. "If the cut sign lies wrong in the wall..."

"It may be enough," Mairi said. "If it is the mark making a crossing."

Calder said, "We do not know the orientation of the symbol matters."

"Then you offer something better."

He did not.

Tam had already gone to the door of the room and was staring hard at the blistered patch as if willing himself to see through paper and lath into the old timber beneath. "How deep?"

"Far enough," said Ailie.

"We cut the paper only," said Mairi. "No more than enough to see. Then decide."

The room objected.

At least that was how it felt. No sooner had she spoken than the tide-sound in the floor deepened, and the wet center below the bed gave a small circular ripple—not water, not exactly, for the shine did not break. But the light on it altered in rings as if something beneath had turned.

Mrs. Kincaid nearly dropped the lamp.

"Quickly, then," said Mairi.

Calder said, "This is lunacy."

Sutherland answered, "It is what we have."

Tam fetched the smallest knife from Calder's case before the doctor could protest, and handed it hilt-first to Mairi.

She looked at it, then gave it to Ailie.

The old woman raised one eyebrow. "You trust me?"

"No," said Mairi. "But you are not shaking."

That was true enough.

Ailie moved to the bedside and, from the chair and the mattress edge together, reached the wall without crossing the wet center. With a care so great it might have been tenderness, she set the knife tip under the lifted paper and sliced a narrow vertical slit no longer than two fingers.

The blister collapsed.

Not outward. Inward.

The paper sucked back against the lath with a damp sound, and from the cut line there came at once the smell of salt, old wet wood, and a deeper colder odor like stone left long below tidal reach.

Ailie widened the slit.

Behind the paper lay plank.

Dark with age. Cross-grained from reuse. And there, half obscured by old lime and rot, a carved sign.

Circle. Crescent. Crossing line.

Only not as Ewan had drawn it.

The crescent lay reversed.

The line crossed from the opposite slant.

A wrong setting.

All of them saw it together.

Sutherland whispered, "Dear God."

Ailie said, "There."

Tam drew breath sharply through his teeth. "Can it be turned in place?"

Calder, all skepticism burned out of him at last, leaned in with professional attention. "Not if it is load-bearing."

"Is it?" said Mairi.

He studied the timber. "I cannot tell from this."

Ailie's fingers hovered over the carved sign without touching it. "If turned..."

"No," said Ewan.

The word came shredded, but plain.

All five adults turned toward him.

His eyes were open wide now, fixed not on the wall but on the wet center of the room. His whole body had tightened under the blanket as if something in him felt the carved plank more acutely than they did.

"No," he said again, weaker.

Mairi bent close at once. "What then?"

His lips moved. The sound did not come. He swallowed painfully, tried again, and failed. Then he lifted one hand from the blanket and, shaking badly, touched two fingers to the carved sign in the air.

Then moved them downward.

Below.

Then, with an effort that seemed near to tearing him, he turned his hand and pushed outward.

Not turn. Not remove.

Push through.

Ailie understood first.

"Not the plank," she said. "What's behind it."

Calder stared at the wall. "There may be open space."

"In a sleeping wall?" said Mrs. Kincaid faintly.

"In a reused wall built over older framing, yes," he said, already thinking. "A blind gap, a service void, a section boxed around older timber..."

Sutherland looked sick. "The room was made against the old line."

Tam said, "Then if there's space behind, the sign's facing inward."

"Inward to what?" Mairi asked.

No one answered.

Because they all knew.

To whatever old shape had been remembered through the house and the church and the sea-line alike. To the joining. To the hinge.

And now the question was no longer whether the marked plank had been set wrong.

It was what, exactly, it had been set to face.

10

What Faced the Wall

No one touched the plank for a full half-minute.

It was not fear alone that held them. Fear would have sent Calder at it with both hands if only to spare his reason the insult of waiting. It was the clearer, colder thing beneath fear: the understanding that they had, at last, found one true piece in the machinery of the wrongness, and that the next act would not be explanation but consequence.

Rain moved against the shutter in fine diagonal lines. The floor's dark center gave one slow pulse of shifting light. And in the bed, Ewan watched them with the strained concentration of a child trying to keep ahead of pain long enough to be useful.

Mairi said, "Then we open the wall."

Ailie's head turned sharply. "Not tear it."

"No."

"Not pry."

"No."

"Not with six hands and a panic."

"Then say how."

Calder was already looking harder at the exposed timber, anger finally giving way to competence. He crouched beside the bed, close enough to smell the old salt behind the slit and far enough from the wet center not to brush it by accident.

"If there is a boxed cavity behind this section, there should be backing pieces to either side. The plaster's been papered over. The lath may be irregular. If we cut too wide or prise against the wrong line, we'll split the framing."

Mrs. Kincaid said, "You say that as if the room's dignity is my first concern."

"No," said Calder. "I say it because if there is a hidden space and it has kept dry until now, the moment we break it badly we may collapse whatever separation remains."

Sutherland, still staring at the carved sign as though it had spoken scripture in reverse, said, "Then make a smaller opening."

"How small?" asked Tam.

"As small as can be managed," said Calder. "Enough to see, not enough to alter load."

Ailie gave him a glance almost respectful. "You may yet earn your boots tonight."

He did not answer that. His focus had gone fully technical now, which Mairi understood as a kind of refuge. Let him have it. Useful refuge was better than none.

"What do you need?" she asked.

"A thinner blade. A gimlet, if there is one. Chisel if not too broad. Something for leverage that is not brute force."

Tam said, "There's a narrow wood chisel in my shed."

"No," said Mairi at once. "No one leaves the house."

Tam opened his mouth.

She cut him off. "Not with the room in this state and the church half-open under rain. Use what is here."

Mrs. Kincaid, suddenly brisk, said, "There's a drawer under the sideboard with every bent nail and orphaned tool this house forgot to throw out."

Mairi almost smiled despite herself. "Then prove the house careless."

They scattered into motion.

Mrs. Kincaid went to the sideboard and began rattling through drawers with astonishing speed for a woman who had spent the last hour white with fright. Tam took the lamp from her and held it low while she searched. Calder opened his case again, not to take out some marvelous physician's instrument, but to produce a small folding knife, a probe, and a pair of fine forceps made for flesh and now insulted by carpentry. Sutherland stood with one hand on the bedpost, half in prayer, half in readiness, looking exactly like a man to whom both offices had become indistinguishable.

Ailie remained nearest the wall.

Mairi stayed with Ewan.

His skin had gone clammy-cool now, not with sweat exactly but with that sea-cold dampness that made her think of smooth stone at low tide. The shell at his throat was more sharply ridged than before, the pale seams along the collarbone gleaming in the lamp like wet shell-lace. His breathing had shortened into quick shallow pulls with the strange pause between them. Every time the dark center in the floor changed its sheen, some answering tension moved through him.

She laid one hand against his chest.

"I know," she whispered.

His eyes flicked to hers.

"I know."

That was all she had.

Mrs. Kincaid found the gimlet first.

It was old, iron-darkened, with a narrow worm-bit tip and a wooden handle polished by generations of reluctant use. Beside it she produced a slim chisel, not much wider than a finger, and a small mallet so worn at the head that one side had gone oval.

Calder took them with a solemnity they did not deserve and tested the chisel edge with his thumb. "Good enough."

"Everything in this house is," said Mairi.

He glanced at her, and there was no retort in him now.

Ailie said, "If you strike too hard, I'll break your hand myself."

Calder answered without looking up, "That makes two of us."

The opening was made in breaths.

First Calder used the knife to lengthen the slit in the paper just enough to expose more of the plank's edge and the lath beside it. The smell deepened as the paper drew back: wet salt, old pitch, something faintly metallic beneath. Not rot. Not ordinary damp. A kept smell. Confined.

Then he worked the gimlet carefully into the lath to the right of the carved sign, choosing a place where the timber beneath felt less dense. The bit turned with a dry complaining squeak. Once. Twice. Three times.

On the fourth turn, resistance gave.

Not with a crack. With a small inward drop.

The whole room seemed to listen.

Calder stopped turning.

"There is space," he said.

Tam swore softly behind him.

The tide-sound below the bed sharpened.

Not louder. Closer.

Mairi felt Ewan tense under her hand and fought the urge to drag him bodily from the room in defiance of all sense and warning.

Calder widened the little hole fraction by fraction, then inserted the narrow probe.

It went in farther than the wall thickness alone should have allowed.

"How deep?" said Sutherland.

Calder withdrew it and measured with his eye. "At least six inches. More."

"A box cavity," said Ailie.

"Or a recess framed around something older," said Calder.

"Same family of trouble," muttered Mrs. Kincaid.

The chisel came next. Calder worked it into the seam where the marked plank abutted the adjoining board, tapping so lightly with the mallet that the blows sounded like someone knocking politely on a coffin lid. Mairi hated the thought and could not stop having it.

A flake of old lime fell. Then a sliver of wood. Then the edge eased a fraction.

Enough.

"Lantern," said Calder.

Tam brought it close. Light slid through the widened seam and entered the hidden space behind.

For a second nothing showed.

Then Calder angled his face to the slit and went perfectly still.

"What?" said Mairi.

He did not answer.

"What?"

His voice, when it came, had been scraped clean of all superiority. "Another plank."

Ailie shut her eyes once.

"Behind it?"

"Yes."

"Marked?"

He shifted, looked again. "I cannot tell."

Mairi said, "Move."

She did not wait for permission. From the bed rail she leaned as far as she dared, one hand braced on the wall, and put her own eye to the slit.

At first she saw only darkness and a blur of old wood.

Then the lantern shifted slightly in Tam's hand.

There, beyond the first plank and the cavity behind it, stood a second timber running upright—not horizontal like the wall-board, but vertical, older, thicker, dark as drowned oak. It had been boxed in when the room was built. Not reused as ordinary house lumber. Left in place. Walled around.

And on its visible face, half lost beneath age, was carved the same sign again.

Only this time it was righted.

Circle. Crescent. Crossing line.

Facing the room.

Not the house wall at all, Mairi thought suddenly. A standing post. The post. One of the uprights Ewan had drawn. One of the pale things Tam had seen under water.

Her stomach turned over.

"This was no repair," she said.

"No," said Sutherland. "It was enclosure."

The room gave a soft inward wash.

Ewan's hand closed hard on the blanket.

Mairi turned at once. His eyes were fixed not on the slit but on the wet center below the bed. The dark patch had spread by another finger's breadth. The boards there now looked less merely wet than filmed, as if a skin of black water lay just beneath the surface and only courtesy held it from rising through.

Ailie said, "It knows we've found the right side."

Calder nearly snapped at her for the phrase, then stopped himself because the room itself was doing too much to support it.

"What is between the first plank and the post?" asked Tam.

Calder, recovering, bent again to the opening. "Air. Dust. Old packing at the bottom, perhaps. Cloth, maybe." He inserted the probe once more, very carefully, and angled it down. "No. Not cloth." He withdrew the tip. Something black and fibrous clung to it.

Mrs. Kincaid leaned forward in spite of herself. "What's that?"

Calder rubbed it between finger and thumb. "Oakum? Pitch packing. Marine, perhaps."

The word *marine* hung in the church-turned-bedroom air like an accusation.

Sutherland said, "The lower store."

Ailie nodded. "A keeping place."

"For what?" said Tam.

No one knew.

Mairi looked again at the boxed-in post. Something about the proportions of the hidden cavity, the first plank, the standing timber behind it, the floor's dark center, the chest beneath the church, the old notes about turning or removing the marked piece—something was aligning too quickly now for comfort.

"Ewan," she said.

His eyes moved to her.

She pointed toward the slit. "Is that it?"

He blinked once.

Yes.

"The post?"

His face tightened. The effort of words had become cruel to him, but still he tried. His throat worked. No sound.

Then he shifted his gaze past the slit and down.

Below.

"Under it?" Mairi said.

His eyes closed and opened again.

Yes.

The room seemed to exhale.

Sutherland stared from the wall to the floor. "The post is set down through the wall line."

"Into the floor framing," said Calder.

"Or below it," said Ailie.

Tam looked at the wet center. "Then the opening's not the wall."

Mairi heard herself answer before thought caught up.

"No," she said. "The wall only points to it."

Everyone went still.

Because they all understood at once.

The boxed wall-post was not itself the hinge. It was the marker. The orienting piece. The thing the room had been built around and the tide-measuring had used as its fixed line.

The actual joining point lay below the bed where the arcs met and the floor had gone wet.

Mrs. Kincaid said weakly, "I liked walls better."

Calder straightened slowly from the slit. "If the post descends into the subfloor—or deeper—and aligns with whatever cavity or structure lies below the room..."

Sutherland said, "Then the room and the church are not merely related."

"They are connected," Mairi said.

Ailie gave a single grim nod. "Aye."

Tam's gaze had gone to the blanket box out in the kitchen. "And the chest under the kirk."

"Same line," said Ailie.

"Or same scheme," said Calder.

"You'll forgive me," said Mrs. Kincaid, "if I fail to admire the distinction."

The dark patch on the floor rippled again.

This time there was no mistaking it.

A ring spread over the sheen from some point below the boards and faded at the salt lines as if the room itself were a basin answering something dropped into water beneath.

Sutherland took one step back. "We should not stay."

Mairi turned on him in disbelief. "Not stay?"

"It is opening."

"Aye," said Ailie, "because you dug the chest."

Calder said, "Then the disturbance at the church and the recognition here are linked. If so, closing one may require closing the other."

Tam's face hardened. "Covering the church ground did nothing."

"It may have slowed it."

Mairi said, "And if this floor breaks while we discuss rates of disaster?"

That ended the abstract talk.

Calder looked around the room once, rapidly now, all intellect bent to the immediate. "We get the boy out."

Ailie said, "Across the center?"

"Over the bed, through the wall-side. The post side is the fixed side. Safer than before."

"You do not know that."

"I know staying is worse."

Sutherland said, "The floor is not yet open."

"Yet," said Mairi.

That settled it.

Together they moved with the quick, clumsy precision of people forced to handle impossible furniture in too small a space. Mrs. Kincaid fetched the chair again and set it at the side. Tam cleared the small shelf from the wall so no elbow or shoulder would catch on it. Calder pulled the quilt free from the lower edge so it would not drag into the wet center. Ailie, muttering under her breath words none of them caught, used the blanket from the foot of the bed to fashion a sling of sorts around Ewan's shoulders and chest so that Mairi could take more of his weight without jarring the shell-ridged side.

When Mairi bent to lift him, Ewan caught her sleeve again.

His eyes went to the wall slit.

Then to the floor.

Then to her.

"What?" she whispered.

His lips formed the shape before sound.

Not yet.

She felt it more than heard it.

She stared.

"Not yet?"

A blink.

Yes.

The room pulsed again beneath them.

Ailie saw her face. "What?"

"He says not yet."

"Not yet what?"

"I don't know."

But perhaps she did.

Not yet move him. Not yet break the line. Not yet while something remained unfinished.

Calder said sharply, "Mrs. Bain."

She looked from her son to the wet floor to the hidden post in the wall and felt, with sudden sick certainty, that Ewan was not warning against his own removal alone.

"He wants something done first," she said.

"That is madness," said Calder.

"Then hear him better."

Tam, unexpectedly, said, "What was the note exactly?"

Sutherland looked blank for half a second, then understood. "The marked plank was to be turned or taken out entire."

"And we now know the plank only covers the post," said Tam. "So what if the turning was not for the plank?"

Silence.

Ailie's face changed first.

"The post," she said.

Calder stared. "Impossible."

"Why?"

"Because if it is structural—"

"It's not house-structural," said Tam harshly. "It's older than the room and set through it. We all know that now."

Mairi looked toward the slit. The hidden post stood there in its boxed darkness, the sign facing the room.

If turned, would it face away? Would the crossing reverse? Would the hinge close instead of open?

Or would the whole house split down its memory?

Ewan's fingers tightened once on her sleeve.

Then relaxed.

He had given them what he could.

Not yet.

Not until the thing in the wall was set right—or not until it was tried.

Calder said, "If you disturb that post, you may bring the cavity and perhaps the floor framing down."

Sutherland said, "If we do nothing, the room may open under the child."

Mrs. Kincaid said, “There is no sentence in this house tonight that improves itself halfway through.”

Ailie took the chisel from Calder’s hand.

“All right,” she said. “Then we stop asking the world for a kind choice.”

11

Turned or Taken Entire

Old Ailie Crowe did not move toward the wall at once.

That was what Mairi remembered later: not haste, but the refusal of it. The old woman stood in the room with the chisel in one hand and the small mallet in the other, her shawl damp at the shoulders, her face lined into that hard stillness weather had carved there long before this night asked more of it. She looked first at Ewan, then at the wet center of the floor, then at the slit in the wall where the hidden post stood dark and waiting behind the boxed plank.

At last she said, "If it turns, it turns once."

Calder made an angry sound. "You speak as if it were a key."

Ailie's eyes did not leave the wall. "I speak as if men before us wrote down one useful thing and buried the rest under God's acre."

"That does not make this sane."

"No," said Mairi. "Only necessary."

Tam was already at the wall-side of the bed, one boot braced on the chair, one knee sunk into the mattress edge, studying the slit as if he meant to force understanding out of old wood by endurance alone. His face in the lamplight looked older than Mairi had ever seen it. Not from years. From one long day in which the agreed lie had finally split and shown its beams.

"How is it held?" he asked Calder.

Calder wiped one muddy hand down his coat uselessly and leaned in again despite all his objections. "The post itself? If it descends through the floor line, we cannot know. If you mean within the wall—boxed, packed, maybe wedged." He angled the probe again through the opening, this time downward and to the side. "There's room enough to either face that it was not fixed as ordinary house framing would be. The plank in front is newer. The post is older. The cavity was left deliberately."

Sutherland, standing at the foot of the bed with the old notes still in one hand as if paper might yet save wood, said, "Then they enclosed it rather than removing it."

"Or could not remove it," said Ailie.

Mrs. Kincaid whispered, "That does not improve the thought."

"No," said Mairi. "It improves the honesty."

The floor's dark center rippled again.

All of them saw it. The sheen across the boards stirred in a faint ring, not enough to break the surface because there was no true surface to break, only the suggestion of one beneath the wood. But the light on it shifted outward in a circle that touched the salt lines and died there.

Ewan flinched under Mairi's hand.

That settled more than argument could have.

"Do it," she said.

Calder rounded on her. "If the post binds the room to whatever lower structure exists, forcing it may widen the join."

"And if it closes it?"

He had no answer ready for that, which was answer enough.

Ailie handed the mallet to Tam. "You've the strength and the least shaking."

Tam almost laughed. "That's a poor comfort."

"It's the one in reach."

Together Ailie and Calder widened the slit.

Not much. A quarter-inch more at one side, then at the other, enough to expose more of the hidden post's face and the old packing around it. Dry blackened fibers showed at the edges—oakum indeed, stiff with age and pitch, crumbling where Calder's probe worried it loose. The carved sign on the post stood clearer now.

It was beautiful in the way old practical things sometimes were. Not ornate. Not decorative. Only deliberate.

The circle true enough that it had likely been scribed with cord or compass. The crescent nested within. The crossing line sharp and slanting. A mark cut by someone who expected it to matter.

Only set wrong.

The certainty of that had grown in Mairi until she no longer questioned it. The post faced the room the way a knife face-up faces a hand that reaches without thinking. Whatever crossing it made, it made inward.

Ailie touched the exposed face lightly with one finger, not reverently but exactly. "There's wear at the side."

Tam bent closer. "From turning?"

"Maybe." She looked at the edges. "Or from trying and failing."

Calder said, "If there is a pivot lower down, it may be pinned above."

"Find it," said Mairi.

He nearly protested the command. Nearly. Instead he set his jaw and worked the probe along the upper edge of the cavity. On the left side, nothing. On the right, a faint metallic click.

"There."

Tam brought the lamp closer.

Set just above the level of the carved sign, half-hidden by pitch and packed fiber, lay the head of an iron retaining peg no thicker than a nail but broader at the top, driven through a side brace into the post's shoulder. Not a house nail. Something forged for use.

Mrs. Kincaid said, "Someone meant it to stay."

Ailie's mouth tightened. "Aye. But not forever."

"How do you know?" said Calder.

She did not look at him. "Because they wrote turn or take entire. No one writes that of what was never meant to move."

Tam held out his hand. "The pliers."

Calder passed him the forceps first, then cursed under his breath and handed over a proper pair of short iron nippers from his case instead. Tam set the tool on the peg and pulled.

Nothing.

He pulled harder.

The peg gave not at all.

"Wait," said Ailie.

She took the mallet, reversed it, and tapped twice at the brace beside the peg—lightly, feeling for looseness rather than force. On the third tap, old pitch cracked with a sound like a dry throat clearing.

"Now."

Tam pulled again.

This time the peg moved a fraction.

The floor answered.

Not with a ripple now. With a soft rising wash beneath the bed so clear and close that Mairi's whole body recoiled before thought could catch it. Ewan's fingers locked on her sleeve hard enough to hurt.

"Quicker," she said.

Calder snapped, "Not too quick."

Ailie said, "Faster and careful are not enemies."

Tam bared his teeth and pulled once more.

The peg came free.

All at once.

He nearly fell backward from the release, iron in hand, and only the bedpost caught him from landing full in the room. The peg itself was longer than it had looked, black with age and salt, tapered, one side grooved as if it had sat in tension for years beyond counting.

No one admired it.

Because the hidden post shifted.

Not far. Not visibly, to anyone not staring. But Mairi saw the carved sign cant by the smallest degree, and heard—somewhere below the floor and below that again—the sound of a held mechanism remembering motion.

"Turn it," said Ailie.

"With what?" said Tam.

Calder was already looking. "There. At the side."

Halfway down the post's visible face, near the cavity edge, projected the worn remains of a small iron staple or ring, mostly buried in pitch and old packing. Not enough to pull with fingers. Enough, perhaps, to catch.

Tam slid the nippers through the opening, jaw-first. They skidded once, then caught under the ring.

"Which way?" he asked.

No one answered.

Then Ewan made a sound like breath torn on stone.

They all turned.

He had lifted his hand from Mairi's sleeve and was tracing in the air with two shaking fingers.

Not the sign itself. Its crossing line.

He drew it slanting one way. Stopped. Then reversed it.

There.

"The other," whispered Mairi.

Ailie nodded once. "Back against the room."

Tam set his teeth and pulled the ring gently toward the opposite slant.

At first nothing happened.

Then the post moved.

Not smoothly. Not freely. It turned with the grudging, resistant motion of something long fixed in pitch and packed silence. A quarter-inch. Another. Old fibers ground in the cavity. Somewhere below the room, beneath plank and joist and blind dark, there came a low wooden complaint as if another part of the same structure had answered the movement in kind.

The carved sign began to reverse itself.

The crescent withdrew from its inward opening. The crossing line shifted off its old angle.

As it turned, the room reacted.

The wet center below the bed did not spread. It deepened. The dark sheen sank suddenly, as if whatever had pressed upward there had been denied the exact face it needed and was now pulling back through itself. The tide-sound rose once into a full low wash beneath the boards—louder than before, close enough to make Mrs. Kincaid give a strangled cry—and then broke into a confusion of lesser slaps and draw-offs, like harbor water turned against contrary current.

"Keep going!" Mairi said.

Tam did.

The post resisted harder at mid-turn, as if it had found some old accustomed notch and meant to stay there. Calder, all his caution burned off by necessity, climbed onto the chair beside Tam and set both hands on the tool with him.

"Together."

They strained.

Ailie drove the mallet handle once into the packed oakum below the opening, not striking the post but loosening the choke around it.

The post lurched another fraction.

The sign reached its opposite facing.

And then everything in the room changed at once.

The blister in the wallpaper beside the slit collapsed inward with a wet sucking sound. The salt arcs on the floor lost their clean edges as if water had run over chalk. The dark center below the bed gave one convulsive shimmer and vanished—no wet left behind, only old boards suddenly dull and dry as if they had never shone at all.

The tide-sound stopped.

Not faded. Stopped.

Silence hit the room so hard it rang in Mairi's ears.

No water. No breathing walls. No hidden wash.

Only wind at the shutter and six living bodies forgetting for a moment how ordinary quiet was meant to sound.

Tam let go first. Calder after. The nippers slipped from the ring and dropped to the mattress.

The hidden post remained in its new position, canted opposite to the way they had found it. The sign now faced away from the room, its inward opening closed off from them.

Mrs. Kincaid sat down abruptly on the chair in the kitchen as if her knees had been privately cut. "Sweet Lord."

Sutherland crossed himself again and this time did not seem to care who saw.

Mairi looked only at Ewan.

His whole body had gone slack.

Not dead slack. Thank God, not that. But the murderous strain had gone out of his face all at once, leaving him white and spent and terribly young. His hand slipped from her sleeve. His breathing, still too shallow, had lost the pause in it. It came now like a child's exhausted sleep on the far side of fever—uneven, but wholly his own.

"Ewan."

His eyes opened halfway.

Not with alarm .Not with effort. Simply opened.

Mairi had not realized until that moment how much of the last two days had been spent looking into him and seeing him look elsewhere. Now, for the first time since the beach, his gaze seemed to rest fully where it landed.

On her.

There was recognition in it. Weariness. Pain. But no divided listening. No terrible attention cast through walls and below floors.

She touched his face with shaking fingers. Still cool. Yet warmer than before, or perhaps only human in the old proportions again.

"Ewan."

His mouth moved.

Nothing came at first. Then, hoarse and raw as a gull-cry ground through sand, one word.

"Ma."

Mrs. Kincaid began to weep behind them.

Mairi did not. Could not. The word had gone into her too deep for tears. It landed somewhere beneath language and steadied her so violently she had to bow over the bed and press her forehead against his hair just to keep from falling apart in front of them all.

"I'm here," she said into him. "Aye. I'm here."

No one in the room looked away. To their credit, no one pretended not to witness it either.

After a little while Sutherland cleared his throat softly. "The church."

Mairi straightened.

Of course. The church. The chest below the yard. The other end of the line.

Calder was looking at the dry floor now, stunned in a way no ordinary success could have produced. He crouched and touched the boards where the wet center had been. Dry. He sniffed his fingers after. Nothing but old house dust and timber.

"That should not be possible," he said.

Ailie answered, "You've been poor company all night with should."

Tam still held the black peg in one hand. He looked at it as if wondering whether to throw it in the sea or wear it as penance. "If turning the post closed the room—"

"Then what did digging the chest open?" said Sutherland.

No one liked that question.

Because none of them believed the work was done.

The room had quieted. Ewan had eased. But the churchyard still held a buried container under disturbed soil, and now they knew enough to suspect the house and the kirk were not merely connected by old theft or reused timber. They were parts of one scheme, or one old arrangement later broken and distributed through practical hands and postponed cautions.

Mairi looked at the slit in the wall. The hidden post now stood with its sign turned aside from the room. The boxed cavity around it smelled less sharply of salt than before. She wanted it closed. Boarded. Forgotten. Burned, if fire could be trusted with such things. Yet she knew already that none of that would be tonight's last labor.

Sutherland seemed to hear some portion of the same thought. "The church cannot be left as it is."

Ailie said, "Nor opened in the dark again."

Tam lifted his head. "Then what?"

Mairi answered.

"We wait till first light."

All of them looked at her.

"Not because daylight is kind," she said. "Because I will not drag my son through another hour of this while the house is only just quieted. Nor will I have half Greyhook rising to bells and mud because we lost what little sense we kept tonight."

Sutherland nodded slowly. "At dawn, then."

Calder looked unhappy enough to argue and too exhausted to manage it well. "If the church ground worsens before dawn—"

"We will hear," said Ailie.

"How?"

She glanced at the wall, the floor, Ewan, the turned post. "Because rooms tell on each other."

Mrs. Kincaid sniffed hard and scrubbed at her face with her apron. "I hate when you say things that make sense after."

Ailie almost smiled.

Mairi adjusted the blanket over Ewan's chest. "Tam, you stay in the kitchen. Reverend, you sit if you can do it without praying over me. Doctor, close that wall as best you're able but don't set the sign wrong again. Mrs. Kincaid—"

"I know my own use."

"Aye," said Mairi. "And it's welcome."

Then she looked at Ailie Crowe.

The old woman stood still as drift-root in storm, the chisel in one hand, the mallet in the other, her face older now than at any point that night.

"What?" Ailie said.

Mairi drew one breath. "Thank you."

Ailie blinked as if the words had struck some part of her less weathered than the rest.

Then she nodded once, gruffly. "Aye."

No more than that. Enough.

The room had gone ordinary again by inches.

That was almost worse than the horror. The lamp burned as lamps did. The bed was only a bed. The wall only paper and old lumber. The dry boards held no false sheen. Outside, rain moved over Greyhook in its own seasonable business and the harbor answered with the common speech of tide under wharf.

Yet nothing was ordinary.

Because they had found what faced the wall. Turned it. And learned that closing one hinge only revealed the shape of the larger door.

Before the night was over, Ewan slept.

Not the strained listening doze of the last two days, but true sleep—the loose, graceless heaviness of a child spent beyond choosing wakefulness. Mairi sat beside him with one hand on the blanket and watched his chest rise and fall while the others moved quietly in the kitchen, their weariness and fear making low human sounds among kettle, chair, and wrapped papers.

Once, near the darkest part of the night, a bell sounded very far off.

One note only. Muffled. From the direction of the kirk.

No one in the house spoke of it.

But none of them slept easily after.

Because dawn was coming. And with it the church below.

12

The Ground That Held

Dawn came grudgingly and without mercy.

Greyhook woke into a rain-thinned grey that made sea, sky, and stone look as if they had been rubbed with ash. The storm had not broken in the night, only settled into one of those long coastal tempers that seemed less like weather than a decision. Water dripped from every eave. The lane was half mud. The harbor lay iron-flat near shore and troubled farther out, where the swell shouldered in beyond the Mouth and broke itself white against the black ledges.

Inside Mairi's house, the back room remained quiet.

That quiet had an edge to it. Not safety exactly, but truce. The wall held still. No tide breathed behind the plaster. No fresh salt traced itself at the seams. The floorboards where the dark center had stood were dry to hand and eye alike, though Mairi had checked them twice before first light and once again after, pressing palm and knuckles to the wood as if she might catch the house out in a lie.

Ewan slept late into morning.

When at last he stirred, the change in him was plain enough that even Dr. Calder, who had spent part of the night in the kitchen with his boots off and his pride in tatters, said nothing for a long moment after examining him. The boy's skin remained cool, too cool, and the shell-growth had not softened or withdrawn. But the divided look had gone from his face. His eyes no longer tracked corners of the room or paused at sounds no one else heard. When Mairi gave him broth, he took it with fewer swallowed hesitations. When she asked whether he knew her, he did not answer with words, but he gave her such a look of weary irritation that she nearly laughed in spite of all.

That, more than the broth, more than the sleep, convinced her some part of him had come back across whatever threshold had been using him.

But not all.

The shell remained. The maps remained, folded in the bread board's shadow. And the bell from the kirk had rung once in the night after the room was quieted.

Nothing was ended. Only altered.

By eight o'clock Reverend Sutherland had gone up to the church once already and returned without entering the house, merely standing at the door with rain on his coat and his face set in lines harsher than before.

"Disturbed soil," he had said. "Visible enough."

Mairi stood in the doorway, shawl over one shoulder, refusing the morning and the minister equal comfort. "Anyone seen it?"

"Not yet, I think."

"You think."

"The rain helped."

"That is unlike it."

His mouth almost twitched at that, but did not. "We go now, before others begin visiting their dead or inventing reasons to pass the rise."

So now they gathered again, but differently than in the night.

No lanterns this time. No secrecy of darkness. No climbing by the back way like guilty things themselves. The morning would expose them if seen, yes—but daylight also gave every motion a claim to ordinary purpose if kept brisk enough. Tam carried the shovels again. Calder had brought a carpenter's auger, a broader chisel, and a narrow pry bar borrowed from somewhere respectable enough that he looked ashamed of it. Mrs. Kincaid came whether wanted or not, with a basket under one arm to complete the fiction that she was on some domestic errand if asked. Old Ailie Crowe walked with her shawl pinned close and no attempt at fiction at all.

Mairi would have preferred to leave Ewan. She knew that. Every mother's instinct in her wanted him nowhere near the churchyard, the old ground, the buried chest, or any other place men had hidden their failures under earth and prayer. But when she told him she was going, he looked at her, then at the folded plan on the table, then toward the door, and laid one hand on the blanket with such exhausted insistence that she understood at once.

He meant to come.

"No," she said.

He closed his eyes, then opened them again and tried to sit.

Mairi caught him. "No."

His mouth worked. No word came. He looked toward the wall slit, then back to her.

The post had been loosely re-covered for the night with paper and cloth pinned aside from the sign. It stood now in its turned position, the carved mark facing away from the room. The house had quieted after that. Ewan knew it. She saw the connection move across his face with painful clarity. The room had been set right enough for him to rest. The church had not.

And he knew the line still ran.

Dr. Calder, standing nearby with the offensive patience of a physician who thinks the obvious must be coaxed into admitting itself, said, "He should not walk the rise."

"He is not walking," said Mairi.

"You will carry him?"

"If I must."

Ailie said, "He goes."

Mairi turned on her. "You would drag him back toward it?"

"No," said Ailie. "I would rather not have the one person in Greyhook the thing has shown itself to left behind when it is answered."

There was cruel sense in that. Mairi hated it.

In the end, they compromised with necessity. Tam brought the small handcart used for sacks and barrels from the shed, padded it with folded blankets and old sailcloth, and rigged it clumsily into something between a pallet and an insult. Mairi helped Ewan into it herself, moving him slowly around the shell-ridged side. He made no sound but one sharp inward breath when the blanket brushed the seam near his shoulder. Once settled, he lay propped just enough to see, the quilt wrapped around him against the c old.

Mrs. Kincaid muttered, "A prince of sorrow."

Tam answered, "Aye."

Mairi said nothing.

The churchyard looked worse by day.

Not because the disturbed patch was more obvious—though it was—but because daylight stripped away the excuse of night's misreading. The place where they had dug and hurriedly re-covered the ground below the lower burial rows showed itself as a wrongness in texture and color: darker earth, torn turf, one edge of the old footing stone exposed where no stone should show itself so plainly among ordered Christian ground.

No one else had yet come .That was all the grace morning offered.

Sutherland unlocked the gate and let them in. The wet grass brushed at their boots. Headstones stood in their rows under rain like stern thin witnesses unwilling to involve themselves.

Tam drew the handcart only as far as the upper edge of the lower section. Mairi knelt and adjusted the quilt around Ewan. His eyes had gone to the disturbed ground at once and stayed there. Not with fear. With that same grave recognition that had become more terrible to her than terror itself.

"You see it," she said softly.

One blink.

Yes.

Calder stood over the patch with the pry bar in one hand, looking like a man who would rather be autopsying certainty than digging through this. "If we expose it again, we do so cleanly."

Ailie said, "You say that each time as if decency makes no difference to the dead."

"It makes no difference to wood."

"Wood remembers better than ministers."

Sutherland ignored them both. "The question before us is whether to open the container itself."

There it was.

Mairi had known the question would come. She had hoped daylight might make it sound less insane. It did not.

Tam drove the shovel edge into the softened earth once. Twice. The rain had made the re-covered patch easier to clear than in the night. Within minutes the old chest top showed again, black and water-dark under clinging soil, the carved sign cut plain on its lid.

Only now, with the room quieted and her own eyes less drowned in midnight, Mairi saw something she had missed before.

The sign on the chest lid was not centered.

It lay slightly off to one side, toward the lower edge, as if not meant merely to mark the container but to align it with some other line or direction.

She said, "Wait."

Tam stopped.

Mairi pointed. "The carving."

Calder crouched and wiped more mud from the lid. "What of it?"

"It is not set true."

Ailie moved closer, as close as she dared. "No," she said. "It's set to point."

"To what?" said Mrs. Kincaid, as if the answer might yet be something decent.

Mairi looked from the off-center carving to the rise above them, to the kirk wall, then lower toward the village.

The line ran not toward the church. Not toward the harbor.

Toward her house.

Her whole body went cold at once.

Sutherland saw it too. "The Bain house."

Tam swore softly. "It's aimed."

Calder said, "That may be coincidence of placement."

No one answered him because even he did not believe the full weight of what he had said.

Ewan moved in the cart.

All eyes turned.

He had raised one hand from the quilt and was tracing slowly in the air—not the sign itself, but the line between two points. Church to house. House to church. Then down.

Below.

Ailie nodded once. "Aye."

Mairi stood very still.

The room had been one end. The church ground another. The post a marker. The chest a keeping place. And both were set along a line that used Bain ground and Bain walls long after the first householder refused to turn the marked plank because sound wood was sound wood and no minister fed children on caution.

She felt sudden vicious contempt for that long-dead practicality. The sort of contempt only a living woman could feel for the dead when asked to pay their postponed bill.

Sutherland said, "Open it."

This from him, who had buried notes and brought apologies and crossed himself in every useful silence.

Ailie turned sharply. "You've changed your mind."

"Yes."

"Why?"

He looked at the aimed carving, at Ewan in the cart, at Mairi, and then at the rows of Christian dead around them. "Because it was not buried to rest. It was buried to direct."

No one improved on that.

Tam set the shovel aside and took the pry bar from Calder. The lid was not locked; whatever iron fastening had once held it had long since surrendered to time and wet. But the wood had swollen and fused in its frame. Twice the bar slipped. On the third attempt the edge lifted with a slow sucking crack like mud releasing a boot.

The sound that came from within was not water.

It was air.

Cold, old, trapped air exhaling from a kept dark that had not seen daylight in years beyond counting. It smelled of pitch, salt, old mildew, and the deep stone-cold Mairi had known on Ewan's skin the night he returned.

Mrs. Kincaid stepped back. "No."

Tam lifted farther.

The lid opened.

Inside lay no bones. No relics. No idol fit for sermon or cheap fear.

It was worse than that.

The chest held a bundle of wrapped objects laid in order, preserved by pitch cloth and packing rather than sanctity. Coiled line, black with age. A hand bell gone green at the lip. A child's carved whistle split down one side. Three flat stones marked with weather-eaten cuts. And beneath them all, fitted to the chest's length, a plank-section cut from some older upright timber.

The sign carved on it matched the wall-post.

And on the reverse side, visible only now because the plank lay face-up with its "wrong" orientation hidden underneath, was another carving: a second line crossing the first, not making the sign a mark or emblem at all, but a diagram.

A hinge indeed.

Calder stared. "These are not devotional objects."

"Of course they are not," said Ailie. "They are keeping objects."

"For what?"

Ailie's gaze moved to the plank-section. "For teaching the turn."

Mairi looked at her sharply. "You know."

"No." Ailie knelt, not touching, only looking. "I know what old women call things when men stop listening. A turn. A setting-right. A closing of ways." Her eyes rose to the chest lid. "And I know enough now to see they buried the instruction under the graves after."

Sutherland said, "So that no one would use it?"

"So that no one would forget it entirely," Ailie answered.

That struck him silent.

Because it was truer than concealment alone. The chest had not been destroyed. It had been kept, boxed, buried, and marked on a line that still pointed to the Bain house. Hidden, yes—but also left findable under the right pressures.

Mairi went to the handcart and looked at Ewan.

His eyes were fixed not on the chest as a whole but on the child's whistle inside it.

The little carved thing was dark with age, one side split, the mouthpiece stained green at the edge by the bell's long company. It looked like driftwood made useful once and then feared for it.

"What is it?" she asked him.

His gaze did not move.

Ailie followed it. "A call."

Calder said, "That is assumption."

"It is a whistle in a chest with a bell and a turning plank buried under church ground on a line to a room that just closed over your patient. You may call it sewing tackle if that keeps you warm."

Tam, still holding the lid with one hand, said, "If this is instruction, where is the rest?"

Sutherland reached in carefully and lifted the pitch cloth from the bottom.

Under it lay one more folded page sealed in wax gone brittle and dark.

No one touched it for a second.

Then the minister took it up.

The seal cracked under his thumb without resistance. The page unfolded in two stiff movements. The hand was not as old as the first note, but older than Calder senior's marginalia and written with a firmness that made Mairi think at once of men who believed themselves practical and disliked admitting fear even to ink.

Sutherland read aloud because all of them needed the words and none trusted silence now.

"'If the lower line be woke by sea-return or by the speaking room, and if the marked timber be found set toward the sleeping wall, then first turn it outward to break the inward measuring. After, do not leave the keeping chest shut, else the line remains seeking. Set the teaching board to its answer and sound once only, then bury not under Christian stones again but sink at the mouth beyond the black ledge, where the water keeps but does not point back.'"

No one breathed properly for a moment.

Then Mrs. Kincaid said, with astonishing clarity, "You opened one thing and not the other. So the room quieted but the line still seeks."

Ailie looked at her with something like approval. "Aye."

Calder was staring at the folded page in the minister's hand as though it had personally insulted every medical text he had ever respected. "Sea-return."

Tam said, very quietly, "Ewan."

Mairi's hand had gone to the cart handle so hard her knuckles hurt. Sea-return. Speaking room. Inward measuring. The note had named their last two days in the plainest language yet given, and done so from a century or more past.

The chest was not merely a relic.

It was the second half of the work.

The old women had known it. The men had buried it. And the line between house and church had remained active because one side had been turned while the other was left sealed under graves like a postponed repair.

Sutherland lowered the page. "Then we take the chest to the Mouth."

Ailie said, "Not the chest. What is needed from it."

Tam looked at the contents. "The plank. The whistle. The bell?"

"The board to its answer," Ailie said. "That'll be the teaching plank. The whistle for sounding once. The bell..." She hesitated. "Maybe only to warn what old line is being crossed."

Calder said, "You say this as if you have done it before."

"No," said Ailie. "And be glad of that."

Mairi looked at Ewan again.

He had closed his eyes, spent by the effort of being here at all, but when she spoke his name they opened at once.

"We go to the Mouth," she said.

One blink.

Yes.

No hesitation. No divided listening. A tired child's certainty.

That settled the rest.

Tam closed the chest lid again, not sealing it but covering what remained from rain. Sutherland wrapped the page and the teaching plank in pitch cloth. Mrs. Kincaid took the whistle into a square of dry apron linen as carefully as if it were communion silver. Calder took the bell because no one else wished to. Ailie lifted the marked stones and frowned at them.

"These too."

"Why?" said Tam.

"Because men who write such notes never list all they fear by name."

No one argued.

The rain had eased to a fine mist by the time they left the churchyard, but the wind freshened from the east, carrying the sea upward in taste and pressure. Greyhook below them was waking fully now. Smoke from chimneys. A man out by the cooper's shed. Two women at the far lane corner in shawls with the look of those who had set out to discuss someone else's business and found weather instead.

There would be no more secrecy.

Mairi knew that now.

Whatever they were doing next, Greyhook would see enough to invent the rest.

Good, she thought suddenly, with a hard clarity that surprised her. Let it see. Let it live one morning under the weight of what it had buried in notes and timber and euphemism.

They took the lower path toward the harbor.

The Mouth waited black between its stone lips, beyond the wharves and sheds, beyond the ordinary labor of fish and rope and village day. Beyond the black ledge, the note had said, where the water keeps but does not point back.

Mairi pushed the handcart herself now.

No one offered to take it from her twice.

At the bottom of the rise, just before the lane bent toward the wharf, Ewan opened his eyes and looked toward the sea.

For the first time since the beach, his face showed not recognition but dread.

13
Where the Water Keeps

Greyhook saw them.

There was no help for that now.

A handcart padded with blankets and sailcloth. Mairi Bain bent into the handles with her shawl blown back and rain silvering her hair. Her son propped within the cart, white-faced and wakeful. Tam carrying wrapped timber and tools. Reverend Sutherland with the old papers under one arm like a man escorting evidence against his own house. Dr. Hugh Calder with the green-lipped bell in one hand and a physician's expression ruined past repair. Old Ailie Crowe carrying the marked stones in the fold of her shawl. Mrs. Kincaid with the child's whistle wrapped in apron linen as if she had stolen something from a coffin and knew it.

The village saw. The village made way. The village did not yet ask.

That was worst, in some ways.

Questions could be fought .Pity could be spat back. Curiosity could be turned. But Greyhook's silence, when properly frightened, was a thing with hooks in it. Folk drew aside from doors and lane corners. Men at the wharf stopped hauling line long enough to stare and then resumed too quickly. A woman near the fish sheds crossed herself and changed it halfway into fixing her shawl. Two boys, too young to know how to pretend not to look, simply stood with mouths open until one of the Reids cuffed them both without taking his eyes off the strange procession.

No one said Mairi's name.

No one said Ewan's either.

That had its own ugliness to it: the village already treating them as if they had crossed one step out of ordinary address and would need to earn their way back into being spoken of properly.

Mairi felt the old anger rise and settle like iron in her.

Good, she thought. Watch then.

They came down through the lane to the harbor edge and along the rough boards of the lower wharf. The tide was in but not full, moving dark and hard under the pilings. The Mouth beyond the harbor looked narrower in daylight than men ever admitted, its two stone arms black with weed and spray, the outer water beyond them pale with broken motion. Farther east, beyond the line of safe work and familiar depth, the sea had that flat deceptive brightness that meant current was speaking in ways the eye could not read cleanly.

The black ledge lay beyond the Mouth, lower than a proper reef at high tide and more suggestion than structure from shore. Old men used it in weather-talk and route-warnings. Boys dared one another to stand there in summer calm. Women measuring widowhood in advance hated the name without admitting it.

Now Mairi hated it too.

Because Ewan had seen it and seen through it.

Tam halted by the wharf rail. "We'll need a boat."

That broke the village silence at last.

"Need a boat for what?" Kincaid called from farther down, voice rough with the effort of sounding ordinary.

Tam turned only enough to answer over one shoulder. "Work beyond the Mouth."

"You'll do no work there in this weather."

"Then thank Christ it's not your work."

That bought them no more silence, only distance. Men began finding reasons to come nearer without appearing to. A line needed coiling. A crate needed shifting. A net weight had to be checked precisely here and nowhere else. Greyhook had remembered how to ask questions, only by posture first.

Reverend Sutherland looked over the wharf and said, "Which boat?"

Tam did not answer immediately. His eyes had gone to the Bain skiff moored at the inside post—the smaller one, broad enough for three men and gear, handled mostly by him now that Mairi's husband was gone. It rode well enough for harbor work and short runs in manageable weather. Not the boat you chose for mystery, grief, and old instructions taken from church ground.

Calder saw his look. "Not that one."

Tam's face hardened. "You have a better?"

"Something deeper in the stern. Better balance."

"And whose?"

Before Calder could answer, a new voice came from the slip ladder.

"Take mine."

Jory MacAskill climbed up from the lower float, cap in hand and rain on his shoulders. He had been on Tam's boat the day Ewan went over, one of the men who had agreed on the gentler lie before they reached harbor. Mairi knew him well enough to know he was not naturally brave, only conscientious in the small daily ways that let ordinary men survive their own shame.

Tam looked at him. "Jory."

Jory did not look at Mairi. That told its own truth. "Mine sits truer in side-pull. You'll want that if you're going past the ledge."

"Since when do you know what I want?"

"Since August," Jory said, and finally looked up.

That quieted the whole wharf within hearing.

Tam took one breath. “Fine.”

Jory nodded once, as if having surrendered the only useful thing he owned to the day and being relieved to have found a price. He went to untie the boat without further talk.

Mrs. Kincaid said softly near Mairi, “They’re coming apart.”

“No,” said Ailie. “Only opening the same old crack from the other side.”

That felt truer.

Ewan shifted in the cart.

Mairi bent at once. “What is it?”

His eyes were fixed on the Mouth.

No—the line beyond it.

The bright-wrong seam of water east of the black ledge.

His mouth worked. The sound came badly, but plain enough.

“Don’t.”

The word cut through Mairi like wire.

She looked at him. At the pale face. At the shell still ridged at the throat. At the dread there now, unmistakable and wholly childlike at last.

“Don’t go?” she asked.

His eyes shut hard, then opened.

He moved one hand weakly from the quilt and pointed not to the sea, but to the wrapped bundle holding the teaching plank and papers.

Then to the boat. Then to the sea again.

Not don't go. Don't go wrong.

Ailie saw it first. "Aye."

Calder, trying and failing not to be useful in a way that sounded like command, said, "He means the order matters."

"Then say the order," said Mairi.

All of them looked to Ailie Crowe.

The old woman hated that. Mairi saw her hate it. Hated it herself, perhaps, more because she knew why it had happened. Not because Ailie knew all. Because she knew more of the old shape of fear than the rest and had less vanity about guessing from it.

Ailie looked at the wrapped bundle in Tam's hands, then at the whistle Mrs. Kincaid held, then at Calder with the bell, then at the sea line beyond the Mouth.

"The board first," she said slowly. "Set to answer. Sound once. Bell if the water takes shape wrong."

Calder frowned. "Set where?"

Ailie pointed.

Not at the bow. Not at the black ledge. At the thwart amidships.

Tam followed the line of her finger and nodded, seeing it at once in boat logic. "Center."

"Why there?" said Sutherland.

"Because if it's teaching a line, you don't lay it at the mouth of the thing and call that sense. You set it where the boat keeps its own balance."

Calder looked at the wrapped plank as if willing it to become an anatomy chart. "What is 'set to answer' supposed to mean?"

Ailie gave him the same look she might give a gull that had stolen a fish and expected thanks. "Likely the way the sign meets the water line. And if I knew that by birth, we'd all have less need of old notes."

Tam unwrapped the plank on a fish crate turned serviceable by urgency. The wood was dark with age and pitch, the carved hinge-sign on its face cleaner now that churchyard mud had been wiped away. On the reverse side the crossing lines showed what it really was: not an emblem, but a setting guide, one angle answering the other.

Mairi moved closer.

There were notches along one edge she had not noticed before—three shallow cuts, then a deeper one. Wear marks, perhaps, from repeated placement against some fixed line or support.

Tam saw them too. "Here."

He looked to the skiff as Jory brought it alongside the wharf.

The middle thwart had a peg-hole at either side where a removable brace could be fixed when carrying heavier loads. Notches in old wood, spacing in a workboat, a teaching board in a grave chest. None of it would have convinced a sane mind by itself. Together it made dreadful, practical sense.

"Give it over," said Tam.

He took the plank and stepped into the boat. Jory steadied the gunwale. Tam set the board against the middle thwart. The edge notches found the peg-hole line with such easy rightness that no one on the wharf spoke for a full second.

The thing belonged there.

Not beautifully. Not ceremonially. Like an old necessary tool hidden away because no one wished to remember why it had ever been made.

Calder whispered, "Good God."

Ailie said, "Aye."

Mrs. Kincaid tightened her hand around the wrapped whistle until her knuckles went white. "Who used this?"

No one answered.

Because the answer was already too large: not a single person, but a line of them. Enough generations to bury a chest and box a wall and still leave the boat-hole and notch spacing in use.

The village had not merely forgotten. It had continued.

Mairi said, "Who goes?"

Tam looked at the boat, then at Ewan in the cart, then at the east water. "Me."

"Sutherland," said Ailie.

The Reverend blinked once but did not refuse.

"Why me?" he asked.

"Because a minister buried it."

"I did not."

"No," said Ailie. "But one of yours did, and the sea is poor at family distinctions."

This almost wrung a bitter smile from Mairi. Almost.

Calder said, "Then I go too."

Ailie shook her head at once. "No."

He stiffened. "I am not standing on the wharf while the village performs a marine ritual over my patient's condition."

"You'll stand because someone must ring if the water answers wrong, and you've the steadiest arm who still doubts enough to be careful."

It was insult and compliment together. That seemed to disarm him worse than either alone.

Mrs. Kincaid said, "Then I give the whistle to Tam."

"No," said Ewan.

All of them turned.

He had pushed himself partly up in the cart, face white with the effort. His eyes were on Mairi.

The word had come thin but clear.

No.

"Then to who?" said Mairi, going to him at once.

His hand lifted. Trembled. Pointed at her.

That took the whole wharf silent.

Mairi stared.

"No."

He did not blink.

Tam said, very carefully, "Mairi—"

"No."

Again the same terrible steadiness from the cart.

Ailie said quietly, "It fed on the shape of the mother's asking before."

No one moved.

The words did not come as revelation exactly. More like an old draft entering a room through cracks no one had wanted to admit were there. Mairi thought of the prologue as Ailie's mother must have told it, of the woman at the shelf speaking level into black water with her dead child in her arms. Of the old note naming sea-return and speaking room. Of love being the wrong kind of door when addressed the wrong way.

Mrs. Kincaid whispered, "Oh, no."

Mairi's first instinct was pure refusal. Not fear. Fury. She would not be made instrument. Would not have her son, the village, the minister, the dead, the sea, all of it conspire to turn her body into some old office she had never consented to hold.

Then she looked at Ewan.

At the dread in him. At the exhausted certainty. At the fact that he had already been used enough.

If she sent Tam with the whistle, it might work. If she went herself, it might work. If she refused and guessed wrong—

No.

The calculation ended there.

Mairi took the wrapped whistle from Mrs. Kincaid's frozen hands.

No one tried to stop her after that.

The boat crew arranged itself with the inevitability of labor once argument had failed: Tam at the oars. Mairi midships with the whistle and the teaching plank fixed before her. Reverend Sutherland aft with the wrapped page and such dignity as cold harbor work permitted.

Calder remained on the wharf with the bell. Ailie beside him with the marked stones. Mrs. Kincaid at the cart handle behind Ewan, one hand on the blanket over him as if she meant to pin him to the world by sheer village stubbornness.

Jory MacAskill cast off without being asked twice.

Tam shoved them clear with one boot and the boat slid from the wharf into harbor water black as stove iron.

Greyhook watched.

No one called after them. No one asked where they were going now. The whole village understood too much and too little at once.

Mairi sat in the middle thwart with the whistle in her lap and the teaching plank before her. Up close the plank's carved lines felt less symbolic than mechanical. Set into the peg line, it made the boat itself feel truer somehow, as if one piece of forgotten work had finally been returned to its intended place and the hull had remembered the alignment of it.

Tam rowed them through the harbor with hard economical strokes.

The Mouth approached.

Crowe's Ledge to one side, black and weed-slick. The post at the harbor lip to the other, knocking softly with current shift. Beyond them the sea opened into that larger motion men called open water when what they meant was only water no longer sheltered by the village's lies.

Mairi looked back once.

On the wharf, Ewan in the cart was a pale shape under blankets between Mrs. Kincaid and Old Ailie. Calder held the bell in one hand and shaded his eyes with the other though the morning was no brighter for it. The village stood scattered behind them in knots and doorways and silent wharf edges, all pretending this was not a thing they had built by postponement and inheritance both.

Then the Mouth took them and Greyhook narrowed behind.

Outside, the sea changed at once.

Not violently. Not with storm. With scale.

The boat rose and settled more deeply. Wind found the open side of them. Water struck the hull with a different note, less harbor slap than body-blow. Tam rowed eastward along the outside line, keeping clear of the black ledge by instinct and old caution until the weathered seam of wrong water began to show itself.

Mairi saw it then.

Not as posts. Not as structure. As a difference in obedience.

The sea around them moved one way. The seam beyond the ledge held another intention.

Its brightness was too flat. Its surface too smooth between small contrary rucks. Not still, but watching itself.

Sutherland said from aft, "There?"

Tam did not answer immediately. He was reading with his whole body now, shoulders, wrists, the set of his head between wind and swell. At last: "Near enough."

"Not on it?" asked Mairi.

He glanced at the teaching plank. "If we're on it, we're too near for learning."

That sounded like old instruction. Maybe it was.

Mairi looked down at the wrapped page tucked under Sutherland's hand. "What did it say exactly?"

He did not have to unfold it to remember. "'Set the teaching board to its answer and sound once only.'"

"What is the answer?"

None of them knew.

Then the boat moved differently under her.

Not the sea. The boat.

She felt a small shift through the fixed plank beneath her hands, a truing in the hull as the bow crossed some invisible line in the water. The board gave a faint knocking sound against its peg-seats, once, then steadied.

Tam froze mid-stroke.

"What?" said Sutherland.

Tam swallowed. "It found it."

The wrong water brightened.

Not visibly enough for a man on shore, perhaps. But from the boat Mairi saw the seam draw itself around them into relation with the fixed board and the black ledge and the harbor mouth behind. A geometry of current. A line of keeping. Not an island, not a reef-body surfacing, nothing so dramatic and therefore less believable.

Only the sea acknowledging alignment.

Mairi unwrapped the whistle.

It was smaller than she expected. A child's thing once, perhaps. Driftwood carved and bored, now cracked along one side. The mouthpiece was worn smooth by lips long gone.

Her hand shook.

Tam said, not looking at her, "Once."

Sutherland added, "Only once."

Mairi lifted the whistle.

The taste of old salt and wood met her mouth.

For one instant she thought of refusing—not from fear now, but from rage that this, too, had fallen to her. The mother always nearest the shape of asking. The body nearest the line of devotion. The one expected to sound the old answer because love could still be mistaken for consent.

Then she looked back once toward shore.

The Mouth framed Greyhook in black stone. The village beyond lay small and grey under rain. On the wharf, the handcart was only a pale speck.

Ewan.

Mairi blew.

The whistle did not cry like a child's toy. It gave one low broken note, rough and sea-thin, hardly louder than wind through a cracked bottle. But the water heard it.

At once the seam ahead of the boat darkened. Not a wave. Not a surfacing. A depth becoming legible.

Tam stopped rowing.

Below them, under the hull, something pale and vertical suggested itself once in the water and was gone.

Posts.

Not one. Several.

A holding place.

Sutherland made a sound through his teeth and did not name God in it.

From shore came the bell.

Calder rang once. Only once.

The sound reached them thin and wrong across wind and distance, but it reached.

And the sea answered.

Not by opening. By releasing.

The bright seam broke. The contrary slick lost its shape. The water around the boat lurched once, as if some held arrangement below had turned away from its old line and let the current take it.

Tam seized the oars again. "Back."

He did not need saying twice.

They pulled hard for the Mouth while the water behind them settled into ordinary roughness by degrees, the black ledge taking back its common danger, the seam flattening into mere sea. No posts showed again. No pale structure. Only weather and motion and the awful smallness of a boat once the world resumed pretending to be only itself.

At the harbor entrance, Mairi looked back one final time.

The east water lay wrong still, but less so. Not gone. Never gone. Only no longer pointing.

And for the first time since Ewan had returned, she understood the old note perfectly.

Where the water keeps but does not point back.

The point was what mattered. The line. The direction of invitation.

When they cleared the Mouth and came under the harbor's lesser violence, Greyhook found its voice all at once in shouted instructions, boots on boards, hands reaching for rope. Men leapt to catch the line. Women called without asking what had happened because they could see that whatever had happened had not yet chosen a shape fit for language.

Mairi stepped from the boat before Tam had fully secured it.

She crossed the wharf half running and reached the handcart.

Ewan was awake.

Not listening elsewhere. Not divided. Only awake, exhausted, and watching for her as a child watches for the one face that must mean home if the world is to be trusted at all.

She knelt in the wet boards beside him.

"Well?" said Ailie behind her.

Mairi looked at Ewan.

The shell still marked him. The cold still lived faintly in his skin. But when she touched his cheek he leaned—just slightly, just enough—into her hand.

That answered more than any of the others could have.

The line had shifted. The pointing had broken. The house might still remember. The church might still conceal. The sea would certainly keep its own ledgers.

But her son was nearer.

Not saved. Not restored. Nearer.

And Greyhook, standing all around them in rain and silence, had no gentler name left for what it had done than truth.

14

What the Village Could Not Keep

Greyhook tried, for the remainder of that day, to behave as if labor were stronger than revelation.

Men hauled fish. Women mended. Children were called in and sent out again. Smoke rose from chimneys. A dog barked itself hoarse at nothing anyone admitted seeing.

But the village had watched Mairi Bain and her son go out toward the wrong water under the eyes of the minister, the doctor, and half its own guilty conscience, and it had watched them return with the boy still breathing and the sea somehow less arranged beyond the ledge than before. No amount of cod splitting or roof patching could lay that entirely flat.

It was not only curiosity now.

It was exposure.

That was the difference Mairi felt in every turned face and interrupted silence when she brought Ewan home from the wharf. Greyhook had long sustained itself on edited memory—on weather instead of witness, on accident instead of pattern, on old women's "nerves" instead of men's refusals. But once a village sees the shape of its own omission in daylight, it cannot go back wholly to innocence. It can go back to silence. Greyhook would certainly do that. But innocence was finished.

The handcart jolted over the lane stones. Mairi kept one hand on the quilt over Ewan's chest, steadying him through each rut and dip. He had not spoken since the whistle and the bell, but some of the terrible outward-listening had gone from him. His face looked emptied out now rather than divided, as if whatever had held him as line and measure had been forced to release enough of its claim that simple exhaustion could have him back.

That, for the moment, was grace enough.

Mrs. Kincaid walked beside the cart like a bodyguard too offended to announce herself as such. Tam pushed from behind without being asked, the wrapped teaching plank tucked under one arm like contraband from his own bloodline. Reverend Sutherland carried the church papers. Dr. Calder had taken possession of the old bell again, though why none of them could have said. Perhaps because a man likes to keep one tangible object in hand when every category under it has failed.

Old Ailie Crowe alone walked a pace ahead.

Mairi watched that and thought: she is listening for what the village says when it thinks the work has gone out of earshot.

And she was right.

At the lane corner by the cooper's shed, one of the Reid women stepped from a doorway with a shawl half-fastened and a face arranged for concern.

"Mairi."

Mairi kept walking.

The woman tried again. "Is the boy—"

"No," said Mairi.

The woman stopped. Because there was no form of the question that would survive after that answer and still be decent.

Farther up, Jory MacAskill stood outside his own house, cap in both hands. He looked at Tam, not at Mairi.

Tam did not return the look.

Good, Mairi thought. Let men wear shame against one another awhile before bringing it to women for laundering.

When they reached the house, Mairi turned in the doorway and said, "Only those already inside."

That kept half the village at bay without her needing to name them individually. Sutherland entered. Calder. Tam. Mrs. Kincaid. Ailie. The rest remained in the lane or on the margins of it, not daring to push but not departing either. Greyhook meant to know what shape this day would finally take if it had to absorb the answer through walls.

Inside, the house felt altered.

Not cleansed. Not safe.

But less actively listening.

The back room remained quiet. The slit in the wallpaper where they had found the boxed post showed ugly and practical in daylight, paper pinned back, old plank visible beneath. The turned hidden timber still faced away from the room. No salt had renewed itself at the floor seam. No false wetness darkened the boards beneath the bed. The truce held.

Mairi eased Ewan back onto the mattress and tucked the quilt around him. He watched her, eyelids heavy, mouth pale. When she lifted a spoon of broth later, he took it. Then another. Then no more. But he did not look toward the wall between swallows. He looked at her.

Each time that happened, something in her unclenched and hurt.

Calder examined him in a silence so concentrated it seemed almost reverent.

At last he said, "The pulse is steadier."

"Say the rest," said Mairi.

He glanced at her, then back to the shell ridges at the throat. "The condition remains."

"The shell." She wanted him forced to call things by the names she had no choice but to use.

"Yes."

"Is it worse?"

He hesitated. "No."

"Is it better?"

Again the hesitation. "No."

Ailie, at the doorway, said, "Then today we'll be grateful for not worse and not lie about better."

That satisfied no one. Which made it likely true.

Tam had set the wrapped teaching plank on the kitchen table beside the church papers. Sutherland stood over both like a man presiding at a family hearing in which every ancestor would be found guilty by luncheon. Rain moved at the shutter in fitful spells now. The weather was breaking up, not into sun but into ragged clearer patches between bands of damp cloud. Through the window the harbor showed in strips of grey steel and black board.

Mrs. Kincaid said what all of them had been circling.

"Well?"

No one answered at once.

Because the word now meant too many things.

Is the room done? Is the line broken? Is Ewan safe? What do we tell Greyhook? What do we admit to ourselves? What must be mended next before some later child pays the postponed balance again?

Mairi stood at the table and looked down at the old page from the chest. The ink had dried brown and stern. Turn the marked timber outward. Sound once only. Bury not under Christian stones again but sink at the Mouth beyond the black ledge.

They had done it. Or enough of it. The room had quieted. The sea no longer pointed back in the same way.

But the house remained built around a boxed post from the old keeping structure. The kirk stood above whatever had once been enclosed and not destroyed. The village had lived generations on reused timber, renamed cautions, and lines no one had dared redraw.

She said, "The truth."

Tam looked up sharply.

"What truth?"

"That the village does not get another easier story."

Mrs. Kincaid drew breath as if to object, then let it go.

Sutherland said, "Mairi."

"No."

His mouth thinned. "You think I mean to ask for concealment?"

"I think concealment is Greyhook's first language whenever the second grows inconvenient."

That landed too squarely for him to deny.

Ailie said, "Aye."

Calder, to Mairi's surprise, did not retreat into neutrality. "There is a difference," he said, "between truth and panic."

"Then define it."

He looked at the room, the wall slit, the shell at the child's throat, the old papers, the turned plank. For once in his life perhaps, definitions failed him with some dignity.

Tam said, weary and low, "What would you have told?"

Mairi turned to him.

This was the question beneath all the others. Not for the village. For herself.

She had thought, once, that what she wanted was the whole thing dragged out bare into weather and witness. Every man named. Every omission spoken. Every page held up to the light.

Now, looking at Ewan, she knew the matter was harder than fury made it seem.

The village did not deserve innocence. But her son did deserve a future. And there are truths that feed on public handling.

She said, very carefully, "I would tell them this: that Greyhook kept old things under new names and let caution rot into custom until no one knew what they were obeying or refusing. That men hid notes and women preserved fragments and both called it sense. That the Bain house was built with marked timber from the old ground and the church buried what should have been sunk, and because of that my son was made to bear what the village had not the courage to face in wood and earth." She looked from Tam to Sutherland to the others. "That is enough truth for one day."

No one in the room argued.

Because each had already been named by it in part.

Mrs. Kincaid said at last, "And the rest?"

"The rest," said Mairi, "stays in this house until I know what it would do outside it."

Ailie nodded once, as if some internal tally had been satisfied.

Tam looked at the teaching plank. "What do we do with that?"

"Not put it back in the church," said Ailie.

"Nor under the house," said Mrs. Kincaid, scandalized at the need to say so aloud.

Sutherland said, "It should not remain in use."

Calder said, "Nor in circulation."

Mairi thought of the boat. The pegs. The way the notches had found their old answering points as if the village had gone on preserving the procedure while forgetting the reason.

The practical horror of that was worse than any sea monster could have been.

She said, "It goes where no one puts it to hand and no one forgets it exists."

"That is a contradiction," said Calder.

"No," said Ailie. "That is stewardship."

Again that word: not victory, not cleansing, not escape.

Stewardship.

Greyhook had refused it once and made euphemism do the work. Now the work remained, only stripped of innocence.

Outside, the lane had filled.

Not with a mob. Greyhook was too disciplined for that even in fear. But with people who had found reasons to pass and stay and stand just beyond impropriety. Men in working coats with no fish in hand. Women with aprons still on. A child hushed sharply by someone unseen. The village had reached the point where silence required witness to sustain it.

Mrs. Kincaid looked through the curtain edge. "You'll not keep them all waiting."

"Yes," said Mairi. "I will."

But even as she said it, she knew the house could not remain sealed indefinitely. The village needed some version of what had happened or else it would build one out of old habits and half-heard words. Worse, it would build one that spared everyone but the Bains.

She would not allow that.

Sutherland seemed to hear the same conclusion moving toward the air between them. "I can speak."

Mairi gave him a long look. "You will. But not first."

That startled him.

"Mrs. Bain—"

"No." She was tired of the title in his mouth. "You have spoken for Greyhook long enough without saying what Greyhook did not wish heard. Today I speak first."

Tam looked at her, and something almost like respect went cleanly through his shame.

Mrs. Kincaid muttered, "Aye then."

Ailie said nothing, which in her case meant more.

Mairi went to the door.

She did not fling it open dramatically. That was not Greyhook's way and not hers either. She lifted the latch and opened to the lane with one plain movement, enough to let the damp day and the gathered eyes in.

The village stood there in clusters and single figures.

Mrs. Reid. Jory MacAskill. Old Duncan Crowe with his hat in both hands. The Kincaids' eldest boy pretending to be sent for twine. Two women from farther up the lane who had no business here but every reason to think of one later. And beyond them, half visible through the thinning rain, others along the wharf and at the cooper's corner and under eaves.

They all looked at her.

Mairi Bain, shawl on, grief in the bones, weather at her back, with no husband to stand before her and no patience left to imitate one.

Good, she thought again .Look.

She said, "You all know by now that my son came home from the sea when no one believed he would. You know Dr. Calder was called. You know the minister and others were with us. You know enough to make yourselves worse by guessing."

No one moved.

So she continued.

"This house was built with old timber taken from older work on this coast. The church kept notes on it and then lost the nerve for the meaning of them. Men found wrong things in the water and chose weather for a better story. Women remembered enough to be dismissed for it. We buried what should not have been buried, boxed what should have been turned, and called that common sense because it cost less in daylight."

The silence deepened. Not offended. Not yet. Listening.

Mairi looked at Tam then, and Tam did not look away.

"My son paid for that silence."

A woman near the back drew in breath sharply.

Good. Let it hurt.

Mairi went on. "There is no curse to entertain you here. No demon for the lane to fatten itself on by supper. There is only this: Greyhook inherited old warnings and turned them into habits without memory. Then it forgot even that much. We have set right one part of what was left wrong. More remains. And no one in this village says again that what happened to Ewan Bain was only weather."

That was when the murmuring began.

Low. Shocked. Not denial exactly, because too many had seen too much in the last day. But the old reflex of a village hearing itself named in its own failures and seeking at once for seams through which blame might escape.

Sutherland stepped up beside her then, just as promised.

He did not take over. He added weight.

"What Mrs. Bain says is true," he said.

That stilled them more effectively than any sermon could have.

Because once the minister says *true*, Greyhook must either swallow the word or spit out the kirk with it.

He went on. "The church records were incomplete by human will, not Providence. I will answer for that before any man asks her to answer more than she has already borne."

Again the village shifted.

Jory MacAskill took off his cap fully. Old Duncan Crowe looked at the ground. Mrs. Reid, who had likely come hoping to measure scandal, found herself instead in the presence of accountability and had no practiced face for it.

Ailie, from somewhere behind Mairi's shoulder, said in a voice not loud but carrying, "And the sea'll answer the rest if the village grows a fool again."

That was perhaps too much and perhaps exactly enough.

No one laughed. No one asked questions.

The truth had not solved anything. But it had changed the direction of shame. That mattered.

At last Mairi said, "Go home. Mind your own walls. And if any of you have old timbers in sleeping rooms that came from sheds, wharves, or work no one now names proper, you speak of it before dark to the minister or to m e."

That sent a visible current through the gathered faces.

Because now the danger was not contained neatly in the Bain house or the old church ground. It ran through Greyhook's practical habits, its salvage, its patchwork, its whole proud economy of reuse.

Again :good.

The village dispersed the way frightened villages do—not in a rush, but in little breaks of movement each pretending independence from the others. A man called for line. A woman remembered bread. Two boys were suddenly cuffed toward chores they should have been doing already. The lane thinned.

Not cleanly. Never cleanly. But enough.

Mairi closed the door.

When she turned back, she found Ewan watching from the bed.

He had heard at least part of it. Perhaps all.

There was no outward listening in him now. Only a child's tired attention and something else she had not seen there since before August.

Embarrassment.

Mairi nearly laughed then and did not because the sound would have broken her.

"You needn't look so put-upon," she said softly, going to him. "I did not ask your leave to shame a whole village."

One corner of his mouth twitched. Not a smile. Near enough to one that she felt the world alter by a degree.

She sat beside him and laid her hand over his.

Still cool. Still marked. Still his.

In the kitchen, the others began speaking in low practical tones about where the teaching plank should be kept, how the church patch would be dressed, what timbers in the Bain wall might yet need replacing in fair weather, and which houses in Greyhook should be quietly inspected before another room learned to breathe.

It was the sound of stewardship beginning badly. Humanly. Necessary as mending.

Outside, the sea went on keeping its ledger.

Inside, for the first time since the beach, the house did not seem to be listening for an answer from elsewhere.

It was listening only to its living.

And that, for one rain-grey day in Greyhook, was enough.

15

The Line That Lapsed

Greyhook did not return to normal.

Mairi understood by evening that the village would spend weeks pretending otherwise.

That was its talent. Not denial exactly. Denial was too clean a word, too singular, too dependent on the idea that a truth stood plainly before a person and was then refused. Greyhook worked by adjustment. By trimming the edge off what had happened until it could be carried in ordinary speech without cutting the tongue. By making room for dread the way it made room for storm damage: with salvage, labor, and one eye turned from the ugliest corner.

So by sunset the lane talk had already begun to settle into new shapes.

Not lies, precisely. Not yet.

Just smaller words.

There had been old timber in the Bain wall. The kirk had found queer things in the records. The boy had been touched hard by the sea but was back in himself some. The minister meant to inspect a few of the older houses. Tam and Jory had gone past the Mouth on some old instruction the church had uncovered. No one was to speak foolishly of curses.

The last of those told Mairi more than the rest.

No one was to speak foolishly of curses. Meaning, of course, that half the village would do just that in kitchens after dark, while insisting they had not.

Let them.

So long as the larger lie stayed dead.

By late afternoon Dr. Calder had gone to wash and return. Reverend Sutherland had gone back to the kirk with Tam and Jory to see the disturbed ground properly covered and the old patch of yard re-marked without deceit and without detail. Mrs. Kincaid, who had earned the right to say anything she pleased, had stayed long enough to bully broth and hot water into the house before going to put her own stove to rights and inform her household that if any one of them repeated a single stupid sentence about Mairi Bain or the boy, she would break a spoon over their heads.

Old Ailie Crowe alone remained.

Not because she was invited. Because she was not yet done.

The back room lay in a calm so ordinary it made Mairi uneasy.

The slit in the wallpaper had been covered loosely with clean cloth pinned back from the turned post beneath. The old marked timber remained boxed in the wall, its sign facing away now, its line no longer cast inward through the room. Calder had wanted to board it before dusk. Ailie had said no, not until they understood whether covering was the same thing as forgetting. Mairi had sided with Ailie, to the doctor's visible frustration.

So the wall remained visibly wrong.

Good, Mairi thought. Let the room keep one wound open where we can see it.

Ewan slept through most of the afternoon. When he woke, he was clearer than before and more fragile too, as if whatever had released him had left him with the common weakness of a body forced too long to serve two masters. He drank more. He spoke not at all, but the struggle to do so no longer showed itself in every attempt. Twice he reached for the charcoal. Twice Mairi refused it. The second time he gave her a look so unmistakably himself—annoyed, intelligent, faintly offended—that she nearly yielded from gratitude alone.

"Tomorrow," she said.

That displeased him.

Good again, she thought. Displeasure is life.

By evening the weather finally began to lift in tatters. Not into sun. Into strips of pale light between racing cloud, enough to silver the wet roofs and show the harbor again as itself rather than as one long bruise.

Mairi stood at the kitchen window with her hands wrapped around tea gone cool and watched the lane.

Ailie sat at the table with the teaching plank before her, not touching it, merely looking as if she expected old wood to betray another sentence if watched without blinking.

At last Mairi said, “You knew more than you said.”

Ailie did not deny it. “I knew the shape of more than the names.”

“That is an old woman’s privilege, is it?”

“No,” said Ailie. “Only an old woman’s burden, if she has any sense.”

Mairi turned from the window. “Burden shared late is half vanity.”

That won a short look from Ailie, keen as a gull’s eye. “Aye.”

No defense. No resentment. Only assent.

That took more of Mairi’s anger out of her than excuse would have.

She sat opposite. The teaching plank lay between them in the dimming light, the hinge sign cut into its face dark and plain. She hated the thing. She respected it. She hated herself for respecting it.

At length she said, “The old note.”

Ailie waited.

"Sea-return. Speaking room. Inward measuring. The little living body quickest led of all thresholds." She looked toward the back room, then back to the plank. "What was my line's part in this before the village forgot it?"

Ailie did not answer at once. For once Mairi believed the delay honest.

"Not your line alone," she said at last. "But nearer to it than most."

"That is not enough."

"It is what I have."

"No. Not now."

Ailie let out a slow breath and folded her hands. "The old women said there was once a keeping household near the lower rise before the kirk was built proper. Not priests, not pagans in the fool way men like to say it, just a house that held the burden of remembering where not to turn grief and where not to set the old pieces wrong. Some years there was work to do. Most years there was only watching."

"A keeper line."

"Aye."

"And Bain?"

Ailie gave one small nod. "Or married into it. Or nearest to it. Such things braid over time."

Mairi sat very still.

Her grandmother had put bowls of brine under beds in storm season. Her mother had refused to let sleeping children lie against certain walls in old houses and had called it draft-sense when asked. Mairi herself had kept some habits and shed others after widowhood, after anger, after the grinding ordinary insult of surviving without enough help and with too much advice.

Not because she had rejected an office. Because she had thought them habits.

The realization came not as revelation but as indictment.

"We lapsed," she said.

Ailie's eyes lifted to hers. "Aye."

Mairi laughed once, softly and without mirth. "There is your honest word."

The line that lapsed.

Not because of one sin. Not because of one villain. Because over generations people learned to translate relation into custom, custom into superstition, superstition into embarrassment, and embarrassment into neglect.

And when neglect finally ripened into danger, it was the child nearest the old line who had been seized into use.

Ewan.

Mairi put both palms flat on the table to keep them from shaking. "If I had known."

"No," said Ailie sharply, "you would not."

Mairi looked up.

The old woman's face had hardened. "You speak as if knowledge is a latch a woman only failed to lift. What you had were remnants. Muttered things. Half-rules stripped of reason by men and ministers and ordinary hard years. Do not take every dead hand's failure and wear it as if it were your own design."

Mairi had not expected comfort from Ailie Crowe. What she got was better: refusal of foolish guilt.

It helped less than she wished and more than she wanted.

"So what now?" she said.

Ailie looked at the plank. "Now Greyhook stops pretending salvage is innocent."

"That is for the village."

"Aye."

"And for me?"

At this the old woman was quiet longer.

Then she said, "For you, maybe the old work comes back by choice instead of through the child."

The room seemed to narrow around that sentence.

Mairi did not misunderstand it.

"That is too neat."

"Aye," said Ailie. "So do not make it neat."

The old woman looked toward the back room where Ewan slept.

"He was taken in because the line had no one standing awake in it. The house was wrong-set. The chest was buried to point instead of kept to answer. The kirk covered. The men lied. The women remembered too softly. He was nearest and young enough to be led."

Mairi listened without moving.

"If the village means not to let the same happen again," Ailie went on, "then someone must keep more than notes in a box and old timber under paper."

"A keeper," said Mairi.

Ailie shrugged once. "Call it what you like. Names are where men begin embalming a thing."

That almost won a smile from Mairi. Almost.

She looked again to the window. The lane outside lay damp and empty for the moment, though lights had begun to show in nearby houses one by one. Greyhook settling itself for evening. Meals. Fires. Conversations lowered by weather and by the memory of what the day had been forced to admit.

"Would the sea take me for it?" she asked quietly.

Ailie's gaze sharpened. "Do not make poetry of what isn't asking for it."

"Answer."

The old woman considered her with the grave impatience of one faced with a question badly phrased but worth answering all the same.

"Not take as in death," she said. "Not if the old note and the old women held sense. But there is a bind in it, I think. A line of acknowledgment. A right setting. A house and coast kept from pointing inward. Not a bargain in the fool way men tell stories. More a continuance."

A continuance.

The word landed heavily.

Not martyrdom. Not sacrifice. Not victory. An ongoingness.

Mairi thought of bowls of brine. Certain walls. Sleeping rooms. Knowing what timber not to use. Knowing what to do with old marked things rather than burying them under graves and hoping the church roof would moralize them into silence.

A life, then. Not an ending. And that somehow frightened her more.

Because noble deaths are easy to imagine. Altered continuance is harder. It asks tomorrow and next winter and ten years of weather and ordinary patience. It asks one to remain.

She said, "You speak as if I have chosen."

Ailie's face gave nothing away. "No. I speak as if the choosing is coming."

Before Mairi could answer, boots sounded on the lane and a hand struck the outer frame twice.

Tam.

He entered with wet shoulders and the Reverend at his back, both men carrying the look of those who had worked hard at practical things and found no comfort in them.

"Well?" said Mairi.

Sutherland removed his hat. "The patch is covered proper."

"That is not what I asked."

"No." He glanced toward the plank on the table, then the back room. "We checked the lower side of the kirk wall and the vestry flooring. No fresh salt. No sounds."

"And the old yard?"

Tam answered this time. "Settled enough."

"Enough."

He nodded.

Mairi read the rest in his face before he spoke it. "And?"

Tam looked at the minister, then back to her. "Jory told Reid. Reid told Kincaid. Kincaid told two others he thought fit. By dark half the harbor knew enough."

Mrs. Kincaid, entering on the tail of this with a pot under one arm and hearing only the last, said, "Then half the harbor knows less than I do and more than is good for them."

Tam almost smiled despite himself. "Aye."

Sutherland set down a folded paper on the table beside the plank. "I wrote a list."

Mairi stared. "A list."

"Of houses likely built with lower-store timber or old shore salvage from the wrong years."

That got her attention.

Ailie leaned in first. "Show."

He unfolded the sheet.

Seven houses.

The Bain place at top. Then the old Kincaid cottage by the inner reach. A disused storehouse near the cooper's shed. Two Crowe houses, one still occupied, one not. The old Reid loft. And a near-collapsed lean-to by the harbor road no one lived in now.

Mrs. Kincaid gave an outraged sound. "My mother slept in that cottage forty years."

"And heard nothing?" said Ailie.

Mrs. Kincaid stopped. Then: "She did hate the back room in storm weather."

No one found that amusing.

Mairi looked from the list to the turned plank.

The village's next labor had already begun to shape itself: walls to inspect, timber to name, marked pieces to remove or turn, old habits to relearn before they were needed.

Stewardship again.

She was so tired of that word. And yet it was the only one that did not lie.

Ewan made a sound in the back room.

Not distress. A waking shift.

Mairi went to him at once.

He had opened his eyes and was looking toward the kitchen, hearing the voices there. When she came near, he looked at her, then toward the doorway, and lifted one hand from the blanket in a small asking motion.

"You want them?"

One blink.

Yes.

So she did what fear would once have forbidden and gratitude now demanded. She opened the back-room door fully and let the others be seen.

Tam at the table with his cap in both hands. Mrs. Kincaid fussing with bowls and pretending not to watch him. Ailie bent over the minister's list as if it were a weather chart she intended to improve. Sutherland himself looking both guilty and useful. The ordinary posture of tired people beginning necessary work.

Ewan looked at them all.

Then at the wall with the turned post hidden behind cloth. Then back.

He did not smile. He was too worn for that.

But something in his face eased.

Mairi understood.

He needed to see that the line had not merely been broken for him and then abandoned again. That the living were taking it up in their poor human way. That the village, if not redeemed, had at least been forced to become answerable.

She sat beside him and took his hand.

"They're staying," she said quietly. "For now."

His fingers closed weakly around hers.

In the kitchen, Tam said, "We start with the empty houses."

Mrs. Kincaid answered, "You start with your own guilty shoulders and then the empty houses."

Ailie said, "No. Bain first. There's still a post in the wall."

Calder, returning at that moment without knocking because no one in Greyhook any longer believed knocking mattered at this house, heard just enough to say, "And after Bain, the vestry."

Sutherland looked up, weary and grim. "Aye."

There it was then.

Not a council. Not a ritual. No village pageant of guilt and absolution.

Only the plain beginning of work.

Mairi sat with her son in the dimming room and listened to them divide the labor of mending what had lapsed.

Outside, the sea kept to itself for one evening.

Not because it was appeased. Not because it was kind. Only because the line no longer pointed inward unanswered.

And for the first time since Ewan had stepped where there was no deck, Mairi allowed herself to think not only of what had been escaped, but of what life might become now that escape was not enough.

A continuance, Ailie had called it.

Terrible word. Honest word.

By full dark, she knew it would be hers.

16

The Mother's Place

By full dark, the house had taken on the shape of a workshop rather than a wound.

That was not comfort. It was only labor given walls.

Tam had brought in tools enough for inspection and repair: hammer, pry bar, auger, lantern hooks, chalk, lengths of cord, a box of mixed nails that ought to have been sorted years ago and never would have been if not for dread. Dr. Calder, having surrendered whatever remained of his wish to remain solely a physician in this matter, had spread the minister's list on the kitchen table and marked the houses by age, known repairs, and likely timber transfer. Reverend Sutherland had produced two more slips from the kirk chest with references to "turned pieces" and "sleeping walls," each maddeningly brief and yet no longer dismissible. Mrs. Kincaid had fed all of them by force and insult. Old Ailie Crowe had sat through it with the dry authority of someone who knew that once men were given practical tasks they grew honest enough to be tolerated.

And Mairi sat in the back room beside Ewan and listened.

That, too, was work.

The old post remained in the wall behind the pinned cloth, turned now so its carved sign faced away from the room. The floor below the bed held dry. No salt renewed itself at the seams. The room no longer breathed with the sea. Yet it was not ordinary. Nothing built over a hinge could ever become fully ordinary again once named. The place had memory in it now—not just the house's, not the coast's, not the church's. Hers.

Ewan slept and woke by turns. Each time he woke, he checked for her first. Then the room. Then the doorway. And each time the same order of safety seemed to settle him.

She thought: he is counting his world back into place.

At some point after supper, when the wind had dropped almost entirely and the rain reduced itself to occasional tapping at the shutter, Ailie came to the back-room door and stood with one hand on the frame.

"He's better."

It was not a question.

Mairi looked at Ewan's sleeping face, at the shell still pale at the throat. "Nearer."

"Aye."

"You may say better if you want kindness from me."

Ailie's mouth shifted, not quite a smile. "I've lived this long without it."

Mairi rose carefully from the chair and stepped into the doorway, half turning so she could still see the bed.

The kitchen beyond looked yellow and worn and human in the lamplight. Tam sat at the table with one elbow braced and the list of houses before him, head bent. Calder was cleaning mud from the old bell with a rag, his physician's hands now wholly employed in the indignity of artifact care. Sutherland was copying something from one of the scraps into a proper notebook, perhaps out of guilt and perhaps out of duty. Mrs. Kincaid was dividing oatcakes onto a plate no one had asked for but all of them would eat. A small ordinary scene, except for what lay under it.

Ailie said quietly, "You know."

Mairi kept her eyes on the kitchen. "Say it."

"The line won't hold by notes alone. Nor by one right turning. Nor by old men fixing walls after they should have done it years back."

Mairi did not answer.

Because she had known since before dusk. Not in words. In shape.

The village would inspect the listed houses. The wrong timbers would be turned, boxed, removed, or sunk. The church ground would be watched. The teaching plank would be kept where it could not be forgotten and not be used lightly. Children would not be laid against sleeping walls. Boats would not cross wrong lines casually and call the avoidance superstition.

All necessary. None sufficient.

Because what had lapsed had not been only carpentry or storage. It had been relation. Wakefulness. Chosen acknowledgment. The old burden the village had translated downward through habit until no one bore it knowingly and so the nearest child had borne it by force.

Ailie said, “I will not live forever.”

“That is not news.”

“No. But it is often treated as if it should be.”

Mairi nearly smiled at that and did not.

The old woman went on. “The coast remembers if people don’t. That is the trouble. It keeps making the same lesson until somebody learns it plain enough to carry.”

“And you think that is me.”

Ailie considered. “I think it was nearest to your house already. I think the boy was taken into it because the line had no one standing in it. I think you are practical enough to hate the work and honest enough not to run from it. That is better than piety.”

Mairi turned then and looked at her full.

“Do not make me noble.”

Ailie’s expression hardened at once. “I’d sooner call a cod a bishop.”

Good, thought Mairi. Better.

She crossed into the kitchen.

The others looked up. Even Calder, who still retained just enough vanity to resent the fact that the evening's center no longer belonged to his examinations.

Mairi stood at the table and laid one hand on the minister's copied notes, one on the house list Tam had been marking.

"When you begin inspecting the others," she said, "this house goes first."

Tam opened his mouth. "Mairi—"

"No."

He stopped.

Calder said, "We have already identified the principal issue here."

"The principal issue is still in the wall," she said. "And the principal issue in Greyhook is that every man in this room has learned to speak of pieces while pretending not to know the shape."

That landed on all of them, though differently.

She went on.

"The post stays turned. The room stays watched. The listed houses are checked. The kirk floor and vestry are opened proper in daylight and repaired. The plank and whistle and notes are kept together under no church lock and under no house floor." She looked at Sutherland. "A record is made in full, not excerpted, not moralized, not cut apart when the next minister grows uneasy."

Sutherland inclined his head once. "Yes."

Mairi looked at Tam. "The boat-holes are checked. Any other fittings that answer the teaching board are named and removed where they should not remain in ordinary work."

Tam nodded slowly. "Aye."

Then she looked at all of them.

"And I keep the rest."

Silence.

Mrs. Kincaid set down the plate in her hands very carefully. "Mairi."

She met the older woman's eyes. "No one else."

Ailie did not look surprised. Only sad, which Mairi disliked more.

Calder frowned. "Keep what, exactly?"

Mairi's mouth almost twisted. "There is a physician's question."

He bristled, then forced himself still. "Answer it anyway."

"The walls. The signs. The old pieces. The house rules. The watching. The knowing where not to turn grief and where not to let children sleep and what to do if the sea begins naming itself wrong again." She glanced toward the back room. "The line."

Tam's face had gone bleak. "You cannot mean to take that all on yourself."

"I do not mean to take it on alone. I mean it ends being no one's proper work."

That shut him.

Sutherland said, after a moment, "And how would you have it held?"

Mairi looked at the old notes, the cut pages, the copied list.

"Not under church authority only. That failed. Not as women's muttering only. That failed too. It is written. It is taught. It is inspected. It is kept in use enough not to rot into story and kept out of use enough not to become convenience."

Ailie nodded once, fiercely.

Mrs. Kincaid said, "Then two households know it at minimum."

Mairi turned.

The older woman stood straighter than her stoutness usually allowed, jaw set.

"You think I'll let you sit with all that alone because your grief is prettier than mine?" she said. "No."

That nearly undid Mairi where she stood.

Not because it was tender. Because it was practical.

A second household. A second witness. Not noble solitude. Continuance.

Tam said, "Three."

All of them looked at him.

He held their gaze, and in his face Mairi saw at last the final movement of his shame into use.

“It was my boat. My lie. My blood. Three households know it.”

Mrs. Kincaid gave a hard approving sniff.

Sutherland said, more quietly, “And the kirk keeps the full record without owning the whole burden.”

Mairi considered that. Then nodded once.

Calder, who had no household claim in Greyhook’s buried line and knew it, looked briefly like a man excluded from an order he had no faith in and yet had helped discover. At last he said, “Then I keep the medical record.”

Ailie’s eyes narrowed. “For what?”

“In case the shell changes. In case the boy’s condition worsens or lessens. In case anyone later decides this was all weather and nerves and old women and there is no account from the body itself.” He paused. “I will not have that.”

Mairi looked at him differently after that.

Not warmly. But differently.

“Then you write true,” she said.

“Yes.”

No one said *agreed*. No one needed to. The thing in the room had already taught them that formal words were less important than right setting.

From the back room came a small sound.

Mairi turned at once and crossed back through the doorway.

Ewan was awake.

The lamplight caught his face softly now. He looked younger in sleep and waking both than he had in days, though the shell remained and the cold had not wholly left him. His eyes found her and stayed there.

"I'm here," she said.

His lips moved.

This time the word came easier than before, though hoarse still.

"Stay."

It was only that.

Not *do not leave me ever*. Not *save me*. Only *stay*.

Mairi sat at once and took his hand.

"Aye."

Behind her, in the kitchen, the others lowered their voices instinctively. Tools were gathered. Papers stacked. The house began the ordinary sounds of people settling to a night's uneasy labor and planning. She could hear Tam moving the teaching plank to the shelf by the chimney where nothing wet or foolish would reach it easily. Mrs. Kincaid arguing with Sutherland over where the copied full record should spend its first night. Ailie saying that if any man put it in a locked box again she would break the box and likely his fingers after. Calder asking, maddeningly and sincerely, whether anyone had ink enough left for proper diagrams.

Human sounds. Living sounds. Stewardship beginning in irritation and fatigue and no grandeur at all.

Mairi bent and pressed her forehead lightly to Ewan's.

His skin was cool. Warmer than before. Marked still. Human still.

The continuance, she thought.

Terrible word. Honest word.

Not a bargain struck at sea in one night of high drama. A life changed by what must now be carried deliberately. A mother not taken by the coast in spectacle, but claimed by staying, by instruction, by vigilance, by the refusal to let her son become the village's forgotten threshold again.

She did not love that. But love had already ceased to be the measure.

When she lifted her head, Ewan's eyes were half-closed. Sleep was coming.

"Will it come back?" she asked softly, though she did not know whether she meant the sea-line, the room, the shell, the old opening, or some part of the boy himself.

His eyes opened one last time. Moved to the turned wall. Back to her.

Then, with the smallest movement of his head:

if left.

Not words. Meaning.

She understood.

Not if watched. Not if kept. Not if the line lapsed again through habit and postponement and men's better stories.

He slept.

Mairi remained in the chair beside him long after the others had settled themselves in kitchen and front room. The night deepened around the house. Wind softened. The harbor spoke in ordinary dark-water knocks and strains. No tide breathed behind the plaster. No salt flowered at the seams.

Once, near midnight, she rose and crossed to the pinned cloth in the wall. She lifted it and looked at the slit, the hidden post beyond, the sign now turned away from the room.

She touched the visible edge of the old timber once with her fingertips.

Not reverence. Recognition.

Then she let the cloth fall back into place.

When she returned to the chair, the house no longer felt like a mouth or trap or measured chamber. Not safe. Never safe. But inhabited rightly.

For now.

And outside Greyhook, under cloud and tide and the long accounting of weather, the sea kept what it kept and did not point back.

For now.

That was enough to begin a life on.

About the Author

David Horn is a veteran, former dispatcher and police officer, cybersecurity engineer, and cancer survivor. Of all those roles, storyteller is the one that fits best. For more than fifty years, he has been scribbling in the margins—on napkins, in notebooks, and in folders labeled "someday" with all the hope in the world. His fiction is forthcoming in- *Analog Science Fiction and Fact* and the Flame Tree anthology *Gilgamesh*. His short stories have appeared in *AntipodeanSF*, *The Pomona Valley Review*, Rooted Literary Magazine's *Garden* issue, ELA Literary Magazine's inaugural issue, and anthologies from Rooted Literary Magazine, Inked Publishing, and Virginia Fantastic. He lives in Colorado and remains grateful for every reader willing to step into one of his stories.

Also by David Horn

Signals from the Edge (anthology, 2025)
The Glass Child (novel, 2025)
Where the Road Parts (novel, 2026)
Dead Dispatch (novella, 2026)
Everything We Threw Away (novella, 2026)

Short Stories in Inkd Publishing Anthologies:

Yay! all queer free and queer (2025)
Noncorporeal IV
Behind the Shadows IV
Detectives, Sleuths, & Nosy Neighbors
Dance When They Want You to Cower
Heightened Anxiety

Short Stories in Rooted Literary Magazine Anthologies:

Rooted in Rite
Rooted in Music

www.ingramcontent.com/pod-product-compliance
Lightning Source LLC
LaVergne TN
LVHW100521110826
845146LV00002B/722

* 9 7 9 8 9 9 9 4 2 6 6 4 2 *